Emerson-Rose Jofille. She wore a pair of designer jeans, with a wide-brimmed hat on top of her head. Her eyes were shielded from the bright midday sun by a pair of sunglasses, which she promptly removed.

As she turned, he realised her long auburn hair was pulled back into one long, sensible plait. It was a stark contrast with the way she appeared on TV, or in the gossip pages of the papers, where her silken locks were usually floating softly around her shoulders, perfectly framing her exquisite features.

Dart took his right hand from his pocket and held it out, giving her a firm, polite handshake. 'Dart Freeman,' he said. 'Current surgeon in charge.'

When she looked up at him he realised her face was devoid of make-up, and for some reason that surprised him. Then she smiled at him, and he realised she was far more beautiful in real life than he'd ever imagined. He'd seen her photograph many times, but could honestly say now that no camera had ever done her true justice. Her natural, radiant beauty seemed to pour out of her as she smiled warmly at him and placed her slim, small hand into his own large one.

The touch of her smooth, soft skin against his caused him to feel a tug of sensual awareness deep in his gut. No doubt this woman was used to having every man around her dangling on a string like a helpless puppet. Well, not him.

Lucy Clark is a husband-and-wife writing team. They enjoy taking holidays with their two children, during which they discuss and develop new ideas for their books using the fantastic Australian scenery. They use their daily walks to talk over characterisation and fine details of the wonderful stories they produce, and are avid movie buffs. They live on the edge of a popular wine district in South Australia, and enjoy spending family time together at weekends.

Recent titles by the same author:

THE DOCTOR'S DOUBLE TROUBLE
A BABY FOR THE FLYING DOCTOR
A BABY TO CARE FOR
NEW BOSS, NEW-YEAR BRIDE

THE DOCTOR'S SOCIETY SWEETHEART

BY
LUCY CLARK

First published in Great Britain 2010
by Mills & Boon,
an imprint of Harlequin (UK) Limited,
Large Print edition 2011
Eton House, 18-24 Paradise Road,
Richmond, Surrey TW9 1SR

© Anne and Peter Clark 2010

ISBN: 978 0 263 21745 2

Harlequin (UK) policy is to use papers that are
natural, renewable and recyclable products and made
from wood grown in sustainable forests. The logging
and manufacturing process conform to the legal
environmental regulations of the country of origin.

Printed and bound in Great Britain
by CPI Antony Rowe, Chippenham, Wiltshire

11707468

THE DOCTOR'S SOCIETY SWEETHEART

For Jo,
keep being magnificent!
Ex 4:11

CHAPTER ONE

'WHY did it have to happen during *my* rotation?'

Dartagnan Freeman was very annoyed. He shook his head and turned to look at Jalak, the Tarparniian village elder.

'I do not understand why you are so filled with anger about this,' Jalak responded.

'I'm not angry.' Dart pushed a hand through his dark brown hair. Usually, he kept it short but as he'd been providing medical care to Tarparniian villages for almost three months, it had grown a little longer. 'I'm frustrated. Television crews get in the way and have their own agenda because ultimately it's all about the ratings and their advertising revenue.'

'They do not do good work now?' Jalak was confused.

Dart closed his eyes, mentally calming himself down, not wanting to offend the man who had welcomed him to the village and provided wise counsel during his stay. 'They do very good work.' He opened his eyes and turned to tidy up the medical hut where he'd just finished a busy morning clinic. He'd been on his own today so everything had taken twice as long and he was more tired than usual. 'The pictures when broadcast at home will inform the public about the plight of your people, on the events that have ravaged your country. A TV crew coming here is a good thing, Jalak.'

'Then why do you do the objecting?'

Dart stopped and put both hands in the pockets of his khaki shorts, his feet in leather boat shoes, a light cotton shirt covering his torso. He hadn't managed to shave that morning so his face was covered with a rugged smattering of stubble. It was hot, humid and he was tired from the clinic. They needed more medical supplies, more medical support, more of everything, but what he didn't need was a film crew, anchored by the latest bit of TV fluff—Ms Emerson-Rose Jofille—to cap off his already hectic day.

He'd seen Emerson-Rose on television before. She'd no doubt secured the job as a lead presenter for a medical health television show by using her father's influence. Sebastian Jofille was a media mogul and it appeared his daughter was more than happy to be in front of the camera, smiling her perfect smile, swishing her long auburn locks around, dazzling audiences with those piercing blue eyes of hers. It was rumoured that she actually held a medical degree but waltzing around a television studio or presenting segments on morning talk shows wasn't helping diminish the long public clinic lists in Australia, it wasn't helping Jalak and his village and it wasn't helping him. At least, that was *his* opinion and he was sticking to it.

No. He was not looking forward to having Emerson-Rose and her crew here, shoving their cameras in his face, asking him questions about adaptive medical techniques. Operating and clinic lists weren't easy in a 'back to basics' environment where they suffered from a serious lack of equipment and supplies. Still, he and his staff were happy with whatever they could get their hands on and the doctors who worked for PMA were *real* doctors and weren't here to prance around in front of cameras.

It might be 'interesting' to the viewers back home but for Dart, having to explain everything he did was simply another inconvenience he had to endure. In seven days' time, his rotation would be over and he wouldn't return to Tarparnii for another six months, going back to his job at Brisbane General Hospital as a visiting consultant general surgeon.

If only the film crew had waited a bit longer before coming, he would have missed the entire thing. He was tired. He came to Tarparnii to help out, to not only help the people of this wonderful country but so he could forget about and escape the shambles he had made of his own life.

He looked at Jalak, the man who had welcomed him and the rest of the medical team warmly to the village ten weeks ago. 'I apologise for my mood,' Dart said respectfully. 'I don't mean to object or make things more confusing for you, Jalak. The television crew will definitely raise the profile of the situation here and no doubt there will be some sort of an appeal where money will be raised and we might actually be able to get a proper generator instead of a third-hand one that always needs repair.'

Jalak nodded, then angled his head to the side and listened. 'I hear the trucks approaching. I must go welcome.' With that Jalak headed out of the medical hut, giving Dart a few more minutes to tidy up before he, too, went outside, closing the screen door behind him. He walked through to the dirt track that worked as a service road to the village, just in time to see the woman who was responsible for his present frustration alighting from the large truck that had transported her here from the airstrip.

Emerson-Rose Jofille. She was quite a bit shorter than he'd expected, probably about five feet three. She wore lace-up flat boots, a pair of designer jeans, which seemed to almost hug her petite frame, a light blue cotton shirt covering her arms but open slightly at the neck. A wide-brimmed hat was on top of her head, her eyes shielded from the bright midday sun by a pair of sunglasses, which she promptly removed as Jalak and his wife Meeree came forward to greet her.

As she turned, he realised her long auburn hair was pulled back into one long sensible plait that hung down her perfectly erect back. It was a stark contrast from the way she appeared on the TV or in the gossip pages of the paper, her silken locks usually floating softly around her shoulders, perfectly framing her exquisite features. She certainly held herself well and he knew she'd no doubt attended one of the world's top finishing schools, and with Daddy's money behind her, she'd more than likely never known real hardship in her life.

Jalak turned and called him over, beckoning him to come closer. Dart put his hat onto his head and shoved his hands in his pockets before walking towards the television presenter and her crew, who were starting to unpack their equipment. He could see Jalak and Meeree performing the traditional way of welcoming a stranger to their village by taking Emerson-Rose's hands in theirs and giving them a little squeeze.

'This is Dart Freeman,' Jalak said, performing the introductions. 'He is our current surgeon in charge.'

Dart took his right hand out of his pocket and held it out to Emerson-Rose, giving her the Aussie greeting of a firm, polite handshake. 'G'day. Welcome to the jungle.'

When she looked up at him, he realised her face was devoid of make-up and for some reason that surprised him. Did it mean that she had a modicum of common sense? That full make-up and fashion had no place in the middle of nowhere? Then she smiled at him and he realised she was far more beautiful in real life then he'd ever imagined.

He'd seen her photograph many times, back in Australia, mostly in the society pages and in glossy women's magazines. He could honestly say now that no camera had ever done her true justice as her natural, radiant beauty seemed to pour out of her as she smiled warmly at him and placed her slim, small hand into his own large one. Why was it that he now felt like a lanky, ungroomed, hairy gorilla?

The touch of her smooth, soft skin against his caused him to feel a tug of sensual awareness deep in his gut. No doubt this woman was used to having every man around her dangling on a string like a helpless puppet. Well, not him.

'Thanks.' Emerson-Rose laughed a little, the sweet sound washing over him, causing him to relax...but only marginally. 'We're so sorry to barge in here and intrude on the great work you and your medical crew are doing with the support of Pacific Medical Aid, but after hearing from a friend about the conditions for the practice of medicine, I lobbied hard with the network to be able to do a story here.'

She'd *lobbied* to come here? Dart nodded slowly as her words started to sink into his mind. When he'd received notification from his PMA contact that a TV crew were coming, he'd thought Emerson-Rose had drawn the short straw and been sent here. Either that or she'd been looking for 'adventure' to make a change from her empty socialite days.

Now, as he stood, looking down at her, shaking her well-manicured hand, he couldn't help but realise there seemed to be more to the woman before him then he'd initially thought. He also realised that he was still holding her hand and quickly let go, shoving his own back into his pocket. The less he touched the beautiful Ms Jofille, the less he heard her soft tones, the less he saw of her, the better off he'd be.

She introduced both her cameraman and sound man, who were unloading their delicate equipment from the trucks.

'Please, come this way.' Meeree beckoned, indicating they should go inside one of the huts to get out of the midday heat. 'You must be tired and thirsty after your very long journey. Get your friends and we can all have something to drink before the rest of the work will be done.'

'We are very quiet now,' Jalak told them as he took his wife's hand in his as they walked. 'On a day of sunshine, we have lots of children and family around. This half-day, they are at another village, giving help. We have stayed to do the welcome of Emerson-Rose Jofille and her friends.'

'I'm sorry to have kept you from your usual routine,' she replied smoothly. 'And, please, call me Emmy. Everybody does.' She glanced not only at Meeree and Jalak as she spoke but her gaze also encompassed Dart. He tried not to be affected by it, tried not to like the way her calm and personable nature was winding its way around him. He knew she'd had plenty of practice in charming people, in getting others to do her bidding. It was what the rich and famous did, for crying out loud, and it was something he neither liked nor appreciated. So long as she didn't hurt or dupe Jalak and Meeree, who were two of the finest people on the face of this planet, then he could cope with whatever the woman dished out.

As they walked further into the village, Emmy stopped and gasped at what she saw. 'It's charming.' She smiled warmly at Meeree. There were several huts made from bamboo poles with leaves woven as screens to make the walls and the roof of each building thatched with straw and reeds like a large triangular hat. Each hut was on stilts, raised off the ground with slatted walkways connecting one place with the next, so people could avoid the muddy ground.

'What a beautiful village you have. I particularly love the gardens outside each hut. Your native flora is very colourful with a subtle, sweet scent.' She'd bent and touched her finger to a delicate bloom, closing her eyes for an instant as she'd breathed in.

Oh, yes. She was one worthy diplomat in these parts. Dart couldn't help the way his mind worked. Emerson-Rose and her crew were going to be nothing but an annoyance, getting underfoot while he and his team tried their best to provide medical attention not only to this village but to several of the surrounding ones. As a main village, people often walked here from miles away to attend a medical clinic. On other occasions, such as today, loads of medical supplies and accompanying personnel made their way via truck to outlying areas where attention was more urgently required. Being in a country that had had civil unrest for well over two decades, it often meant that medical help had to be sent out rather than people coming to them.

He had stayed behind to continue doing the regular morning clinic but also to be on hand to welcome Ms Jofille and her band of merry men. He looked over the crew as he stood back and waited for them all to remove their shoes before traipsing into Meeree and Jalak's hut, hoping they weren't going to make things difficult.

Some of the young children came running over, the meaning of the guttural chatter of their native tongue completely lost on the newcomers. A few of the children hugged Dart around his legs. One little boy of about two put up his hands, begging Dart to pick him up. He smiled down at the child and scooped him up in one easy move, the thin arms going around Dart's neck as though the little boy was both excited and scared to be so high in the air. Emmy was momentarily captivated by the sight.

He was tall, easily six feet five, and by far the tallest man here, given that the native Tarparniian adults didn't seem to grow above five feet ten, or so it seemed. Emmy watched the way he treated the children with an open friendliness, nearly tripping over her own feet at the natural smile he gave the child he was holding. It completely changed his features.

His deep brown eyes sparkled with delight and happiness, his face broke from the firm, polite mask he'd worn when he'd greeted her and his entire stance seemed to relax with the child's arms around his neck. He also looked very...natural, being surrounded by children, and she idly wondered whether he was married with a gaggle of his own.

Even now, as he stayed just outside the hut, allowing everyone else to gather inside, Emmy had the feeling that Dart Freeman wasn't at all happy to have her and her crew here in the small village. He hadn't said anything but she'd become an expert at reading body language during her years in public life. People often said one thing but their bodies conveyed another. Well, he'd just have to like it or lump it because for the next week, she and her film crew were determined to throw some light on the serious difficulties of bringing medical care to this country.

After talking to her good friend Eden Montgomery about Tarparnii and the challenges the medics working with PMA often faced, Emmy had decided to use her 'popularity', for want of a better word, to do something positive about it. It hadn't been easy convincing the network to go for the idea but as she'd inherited her father's keen business sense as well as her mother's ability to charm people, she'd been able to pull it off.

Emmy turned her head, purposely looking away from the gorgeous Dart Freeman, especially as he'd now picked up another moppet and had one in each arm, others still staying safely by his feet with their wide brown eyes, thin little arms and extended abdomens watching the newcomers with curiosity.

It didn't matter that she'd got the feeling that the tall surgeon didn't really care for her being here, crew included—she had a job to do and she was going to do it. Meeree was still waiting patiently for all of them to crowd into her hut. One of the children, no older than three, was lining up all the shoes by the door, keeping them nice and straight.

'K'tooruh loves to keep the shoes all in a line,' Meeree said to Emmy. 'It is her thing.'

Emmy nodded, making a mental note to get some footage of K'tooruh doing her 'thing', and doing her best to ignore the tall surgeon, who was still just standing there, children around him watching them all. Dart Freeman's gaze was still hot on her and was starting to unnerve her a little. She took a deep, calming breath. She'd been raised in the spotlight, used to all eyes watching her, and it took quite a bit to unnerve her. So why was this tall, dark and handsome surgeon having such an effect on her?

'QaH!'

At the loud guttural shout, Dart instantly turned and carefully put the two children he was holding on the ground. There was no one around but from the long bushland area surrounding the village they could hear the sound of footsteps drawing nearer, heavy on the sodden ground.

'Dok-ter.' The sound came again and this time, Dart managed to pick the direction, heading towards it.

'NuqneH?' he called, urgency in his tone, needing to know what was wrong.

Emmy watched as a man came bursting into the open space of the village, his dark face contorted in pain and exhaustion, his right hand, wrapped in a bloodied cloth, clutched to his chest. She didn't need a translator to tell her what was going on and was glad she hadn't started taking off her boots yet. She left the rest of her crew and followed Dart as he led the man to the hut that had a big red cross on the outside.

'What can I do to help?' she asked, bending

to take off her shoes but then realising Dart still had his on. She straightened, realising that despite local custom shoes were always worn in a hospital environment where disease and infection were present. Looking around, she saw there were two stretchers propped off the floor with bamboo criss-cross frames. There were open shelves containing various medicines and equipment, as well as a large pile of blankets and sheets. It was well stocked and neatly organised. Next to it in the corner was a table, which held a large washing bowl with a small folded towel beside it. There was a bucket of water on the floor beneath the table.

Dart glanced over at her briefly, before turning his attention back to the man, who was still wailing in pain. After seating the man on the stretcher, Dart went to the shelves and withdrew a needle and a vial of liquid, obviously some sort of painkiller. He didn't even bother to swab the area but injected it straight away, soothing the man as best he could, given that Tarparnese didn't sound soothing at the best of times.

'What can I do to help?' Emmy asked again, coming further into the room.

Dart turned and took a sheet from the shelf

next to her, before ripping it up into strips. 'Stay out of my way,' he muttered. Next he stalked the small distance to the table and poured some water from the bucket into the bowl. It was obvious he needed to clean the wound and deciding it might be better to ignore his instruction, Emmy scanned the shelves and found some disinfectant. She brought it over and placed it on the table without a word. Then she found some sutures and bandages, putting them on the small work area that was near each stretcher.

Dart didn't say anything else but, after washing his own hands, pulled on a pair of gloves and unwrapped the bloodied hand. 'Just a gash,' he said, more to himself than to anyone else. He translated his words to Hunklu, his patient. 'An honourable gash.' As he continued to debride the wound site, Emmy stood next to him, assisting him without a word, easily anticipating his needs. She had the locking forceps ready with the suture needle clamped firmly in place when he turned to look for it. They worked in silence and only after Hunklu's hand had been sutured and cleanly bandaged did Dart speak.

'I could have coped.'

'I have no doubt, but you didn't need to. I am

a qualified doctor.' There was just the briefest hint of annoyance in her tone but Emmy had been schooled years ago to always keep her emotions under control. Still, she wanted to make her point.

'Hmm.'

'Qualified to work here in Tarparnii as well. PMA approved. Signed, sealed and delivered to your door, Dr Freeman.'

Dart's answer to this was to raise his eyebrows as he disposed of the bloodied rubbish. He said a few words to Hunklu then sat him up and helped the man to remove his torn and stained shirt. 'Ms Jofille, if you'd like to ask Meeree for one of Jalak's shirts, that will be helpful.'

'It's *Dr* Jofille, if you don't mind,' she said pointedly, her frustration at his indifference starting to affect her. Hands placed firmly on her hips, she almost dared him to challenge her on the point. Why did it feel as though she was on the back foot again? In everything she'd ever done, from being a part of the Jofille family, going to medical school, to her current job, she'd always had to prove herself over and over, and after thirty-two years, she was getting sick of it!

After the briefest of nods from the insufferable

Dart Freeman, Emmy turned and headed out of the hut, making sure the mosquito screen door was shut behind her. Meeree was walking towards her and after quickly relaying Dr Freeman's request, Emmy headed back into the makeshift hospital.

'Where is it?' Dart asked.

'Meeree is bringing it,' she said, once more calm and in control. She crossed to the patient's side, smiling warmly. She decided that if Dart Freeman wanted to be brisk and annoyed with her—for whatever reason, that didn't mean the patient should suffer. 'Hello. I'm Emmy,' she said. The patient was lying down now, a light blanket covering him even though the air was sticky and humid outside.

'Hunklu doesn't speak English,' Dart muttered as he administered an injection of antibiotics.

'He doesn't have to,' Emmy remarked, a touch of haughtiness in her tone as she continued to smile down at the man. She'd been visiting sick people in hospital since the age of eight years, her parents raising her to be a dutiful patroness of different charities and organisations. The fact that she'd followed in her grandmother's footsteps and gone into the medical profession was something neither of her parents had expected or understood but, then, Emmy had come to realise that in doing the unexpected she often unwrapped another layer of who she really was deep down inside. Perhaps one day she would be content and eventually come to like herself just as she was.

'The barrier of language is irrelevant where a kind-hearted smile can mean a thousand words.' She spoke softly, taking the man's free hand in hers in a gesture of reassurance.

Dart watched closely as his patient did indeed start to relax, smiling back at the pretty redhead who, at some point, had removed her hat. There were wisps of the auburn strands here and there, some having come loose during her long day travelling. Her blue eyes were bright and filled with compassion as she continued to smile at their patient. There were no cameras around and she was still giving this man all her attention. Was the show for his sake or was she genuine?

When the man asked something in Tarparnese, she glanced at Dart, waiting for a translation.

'Er...' Dart frowned, trying to decipher in his mind what the man had just said. In truth, he hadn't been listening properly. Instead he'd been intently watching Emerson-Rose, still amazed that the woman he'd seen on television and in the media was now standing here in this hut in the middle of a Tarpanese village, miles from Australia. She had beauty and brains—a lethal combination. He asked Hunklu to repeat the sentence then nodded.

'He would like for you to stay until he falls asleep.'

'Oh.' She smiled down at Hunklu and nodded. 'Of course I'll stay.' Without looking up, she ordered softly, 'Bring me a chair and I'll sit by his side.'

Dart was stunned to receive such a command but there was something in her tone that made him obey instantly and that perplexed him even more. After that, he headed out to see what was taking Meeree so long with getting one of Jalak's shirts, but once outside the hut he raked a hand through his hair and shook his head.

Emerson-Rose Jofille had been in the village all of half an hour and already she was acting as though she owned the place. The rich always thought they were more important than everyone else in the world. He'd learned that lesson at a very young age. What the rich wanted, they took, and without care or thought to anyone else.

Dart clenched his teeth. That simply wasn't going to happen here, in this village, with these wonderful people. If the society princess wanted to be waited on hand and foot, giving out orders and expecting people to bow and scrape to her, she had another think coming. He squared his shoulders, knowing he was just the man to put Ms High-and-Mighty Jofille back in her place.

CHAPTER TWO

WHEN the rest of the medical team returned to the village just after two o'clock that afternoon, Dart was more than grateful to have other people around. Emerson-Rose Jofille and her crew had already started filming, taking some footage of Hunklu in the medical hut, and were planning to cause further disruption to his day by insisting on filming the afternoon clinic, which was due to start in less than an hour.

As the medical team alighted from the cargo trucks, which were their main form of transport, Emerson's crew were there to make a nuisance of themselves, filming the arrival of the trucks and the way they lugged and unloaded the supplies back to the medical and storage huts.

'Busy morning?' Gloria, one of the PMA nurses, asked as she nodded to where Emerson and her crew were talking.

'The clinic was hectic but I coped.'

Gloria gave him a confused look for a moment

then laughed. 'Of course you coped. You're Dartagnan Freeman. Man who can cope with anything. Silly, I was talking about the big celebrity who's come here to film us and make us all into superstars. You simply must introduce us.' The nurse pushed her hair back from her face and struck a pose. 'How do I look?'

'Sensational,' Rick, Gloria's husband, remarked as he walked up to where she and Dart were standing. 'So that's her, eh?' Rick took a good look. 'Woo-eee, that woman is gorgeous. The TV screen does not do her justice.'

Dart looked over to where Emerson was standing, the sunlight shining down on her as though she'd been perfectly lit by a Hollywood photographer. Although she wore a hat, the sunlight still picked up the dazzling colours of her long plaited hair, her skin seemed to shimmer like bronze and her eyes, not hidden beneath sunglasses, were bright as she laughed at something her cameraman had said.

The tinkling sound floated through the air and settled over him like a heartfelt sigh, so warm and comforting. The woman was captivating, more so than he'd expected, and realising that only made the need to keep his distance stronger.

Dart immediately shook his head, clearing away the fuzziness.

'She's way prettier in person, don't you think, Dart?' Rick continued, still staring in Emerson's direction.

'Hey!' Gloria punched her husband's arm in mock indignation.

'You're even more gorgeous,' Rick quickly amended. 'And you're the woman who stole my heart. It's not for sale.' Rick kissed his wife and Dart, for one split second, envied them their closeness. He'd felt closeness like that before, before his world had been torn apart. He straightened his shoulders and focused his thoughts. Now was not the time to be dwelling on the past.

'As you're both so eager to have Ms Jofille make you into superstars, feel free to have her follow you around during afternoon clinic. It'll be one way to keep her and her crew out of my hair.'

Rick raised an eyebrow at his friend. 'You really don't want them here? They're doing good work, taking news of the situation here back to Australia.'

'Maybe.' Dart's brow puckered in a frown. TV crews had come to Tarparnii before, full of talk about the difference their footage would make, but few had succeeded to actually deliver on those promises. 'So long as they don't get underfoot.' Which, in his opinion, Emerson already had. He still couldn't believe the way she'd ordered him about, or the way he'd simply done her bidding. His frown was still in place as he watched Emerson walk towards them, charmingly introducing herself to Gloria and Rick.

'Welcome to the village. We're so happy to have you here,' Gloria gushed. 'And can I just say that you're so much prettier in person.'

'*Much* prettier,' Rick agreed with his wife.

'Why thank you. That's so sweet.' Emerson smiled at them both then turned to glance at Dart. Her blue eyes were bright and welcoming, such a perfect blue in colour, like the sky on a cloudless day. He could understand why so many people seemed hypnotised by her. She really was captivatingly beautiful.

Dart cleared his throat and shoved his hands firmly into his pockets, needing to put some distance between himself and any potential captivation. 'Excuse me. I need to go and check on Hunklu.' With that he turned on his heel and headed off.

'Let me introduce you to the rest of the team,'

Gloria said, and Emmy allowed herself to be brought over to where a group of people were standing by the food hut, having a drink and something to eat.

She only glanced once at Dart Freeman's retreating back, wondering what on earth she'd done to deserve his disdain. She couldn't fault his manners, he'd been as polite as was called for, but it was clear he wasn't at all happy to have her and her crew here. Well, that was his problem and she only had to put up with him for the next week. Once her filming commitments were done, she could return to Sydney and forget all about the tall, dark and irritable Dart Freeman.

As Gloria introduced her to the team, Emmy was surprised to find them a mixture of Australians, New Zealanders and Tarparniians.

'This is Sue, our head nurse. Belhara, our main anaesthetist, Bel, one of our great surgical nurses, P'Ko-lat, who does a lot of our peacekeeping.' Gloria laughed. 'Uh, that's like our reception work. She makes sure we don't get flooded with patients and does basic triage, ensuring those who need our care urgently receive it.'

Emmy shook hands with everyone, eager to hear their impressions of the medical work PMA

was doing in Tarparnii. She was also surprised to
learn that Bel and Belhara had been raised in this
very village and had been taught their skills by
PMA staff who had visited over the years, before
being sponsored to do their official qualifications
in Australia, returning home once they had been
achieved.

'Tarvon,' Gloria continued, pointing to the medical hut where Dart and another Tarparniian were
coming out of the medical hut, 'is over there, talking to Dart. Tarvon will be taking over as PMA
medical leader at the end of the week when Dart
heads back to Australia.'

'Dart's heading back?' Emmy looked towards
where Dart and Tarvon stood on the top step leading up to the hut, both men deep in discussion,
Dart pointing to where the clinic tents were set
up, Tarvon nodding in agreement.

Even just watching them, Emmy could tell exactly who was in charge here. Dart's presence was
very strong and commanding. It wasn't simply
because he was the tallest person in the entire
village but the way he held himself. His back and
broad shoulders were straight, indicating power.
His firm, tanned arms were direct as he continued to point out what he wanted. His stance was

relaxed, letting Emmy know he was a man comfortable with his own opinions and the responsibilities he had to his team. She unconsciously licked her lips.

'Dart's three-month stint here in Tarparnii ends then.' Gloria's words broke into Emmy's thoughts. She turned her attention back to Gloria and the rest of the staff. 'PMA doesn't let us work more than twelve weeks at any one time, mainly because the work is so full on that after twelve weeks you need to return to your regularly scheduled programming.' Gloria laughed at her words, as did the rest of the non-Tarparniian team, nodding in agreement.

'It's good that PMA takes such good care of its workers,' Emmy said, making a note to mention that in her programme. 'So what happens next?' Gloria, Sue and the rest of the team gave her a rundown of the ins and outs of what to expect at the clinic.

Far off in the distance there was a loud rumbling noise and Emmy frowned as she looked around, but no one else seemed to notice anything.

'Is there a thunderstorm coming?'

'No.' Dart spoke from behind her and Emmy turned round, a little startled to find him there.

For some inexplicable reason her body seemed to tingle with awareness at his nearness but she quickly ignored such a sensation, telling herself she must be getting tired.

Emmy looked up at the sky but couldn't see any dark clouds gathering. 'There it is again. That noise. It's like thunder.'

Dart stood next to her and looked up at the sky, frowning and no doubt wondering if she was completely loony. 'Oh, that,' he said a moment later, and to her surprise it appeared there was a slight smile twitching at his lips though he quickly brought it under control.

'That's the people from other villages, coming to the clinic. They can make quite a noise on their way here. Sometimes they do it because they're simply excited to be receiving medical care. Other times they do it to let the soldiers know that they are civilians, not guerrilla fighters.'

At the mention of the soldiers, Emmy couldn't help the shudder that passed through her.

'Problem?' Dart asked as the rest of the medical staff started to break off, each heading to go through final preparations before the next clinic started. Within a few seconds, Emmy found herself alone with Dart.

'No. There's no problem.' She met his deep brown gaze and was once again startled by the disdain she saw there. Was it for her personally? Or for the cameras she'd brought into the village? She wasn't quite sure. Either way, she had a job to do and she was going to do it, with or without Dart's help. 'It's just that out here it really is another world.'

'Same planet, different way of living.' Dart agreed, before greeting a woman who walked towards them. 'Have you met P'Ko-lat, Ms Jofille?'

Emmy smiled warmly at the other woman. 'Yes, we have met. I understand P'Ko-lat is crowd control as far as the clinic goes.'

Dart was impressed with the way Emmy pronounced P'Ko-lat's name. 'Correct. P'Ko-lat speaks a bit of English and so should be able to help if you need a translator. That way you won't need to bother anyone else while the clinic is on.' With that, he turned and spoke to the receptionist in Tarparnese, and Emmy felt as though Dart had once more pushed her away and shoved her into a little box marked 'Nuisance'. That's all she was to him, like an annoying mosquito buzzing around. Well, she wasn't going to let him swat her out of the way so easily. She squared her shoulders and when he'd finished talking to P'Ko-lat, she spoke clearly.

'As I've already mentioned, Dr Freeman, I am licensed with PMA to—'

'Work here,' he finished for her, the thundering crowds who were headed their way starting to appear through the surrounding trees into the village clearing. 'I remember, but until you understand the way clinics are run, you're useless to me.'

He turned and without another word headed towards the clinic tents where P'Ko-lat and Dr Tarvon were starting to accept the first patients. Emmy couldn't believe the pain that seared her heart at his words and closed her eyes in an effort to try and control the rising helplessness that was starting to assail her.

She was *useless* to him? She'd been useless to her father, to her mother, to society at large for most of her adult life. Being born into a privileged family meant she'd had certain expectations placed on her at a very young age. Her older brother, Tristan, may have been under enormous pressure to succeed, to be moulded as their father saw fit, but as a female Emmy's one role had been pretty hostess. When she'd refused to simply be the debutante her parents had wanted and had instead enrolled in medical school, she'd been declared *useless*.

Dragging in a deep breath, Emmy opened her eyes and forced her emotions back under control, determined not to let Dart get to her. He may have a job to do in providing medical care to these people but she also had a job to do and she wasn't going to let him diminish her role or her professionalism by brushing her aside.

'Hey, Emmy!' Gloria called, waving to her and Emmy pasted on a smile and headed towards the bubbly nurse. 'Dart said to stick with either Rick or myself for this clinic.'

'Is he always so brisk?' The question was out of her mouth before she could stop it, and she received a surprised look from Gloria.

'Dart? No. He's very organised and fair.' Gloria headed into a small treatment area that consisted of a table with a sheet over it, a wash basin on the side and plenty of towels and bandages. 'Action stations,' she said as Rick brought through the first patient.

In the first hour the TV crew managed to get a lot of good footage but as her crew was busy, Emmy felt very much like the third wheel. Instead, she watched the way Gloria and Rick worked together as a harmonious team, treating their patients and moving them along to make way for the next person who required attention.

Once the patients had been seen, they were directed to the food hut, where Meeree and a lot of the village women were providing a 'recovery' aspect to treatment. People could sit, have something to eat and drink and chat. Unfortunately, as Emmy didn't speak the language, she felt very left out.

'Ms Jofille.' She turned as she heard Dart call her name. 'If you've nothing better to do, come over here and help me out.'

Emmy ignored his impatient tone and headed to where he was leading a patient into his small clinic area, happy to be allowed to actually do something.

'Wash your hands.' He pointed to the wash basin as he helped his pregnant female patient lie down on the examination table. Dart spoke in Tarparnese to the woman, who was crying. 'Iodine, gauze, bandages,' he said to Emmy as he hooked his stethoscope into his ears and listened to the woman's abdomen.

Emmy's eyes widened. 'Are you going to perform a C-section here?' She quickly hunted around among the supplies for the things he'd requested. In the medical hut where she had assisted Dart in suturing Hunklu's wound, things had been more organised. Here she had to look in containers, lifting lids and digging around to find what she needed.

'She has a cut to her left foot. Stepped on something sharp and is worried the cut is going to affect the baby. I'm reassuring her the baby is just fine and then we'll start on the foot.' Dart switched back into Tarparnese as he spoke to the woman. The relief that washed over the woman's face when she was told her baby was fine made Emmy's heart melt. This woman cared so much for her unborn child that she'd risked walking goodness only knew how far in order to receive medical attention.

Emmy continued to assist Dart for the rest of the afternoon, pleased to be able to help out, even if it was only in a small way. She'd always been a fast learner and had picked up a few key phrases, and by the time the clinic started to wind down, she was able to call a patient in and say farewell in Tarparnese.

'Impressive,' Dart said as he started to tidy up the area they'd been working in.

Emmy smiled brightly, thrilled that he'd noticed her attempts to help and adapt. That was why he'd made the comment, right? She shook her confusion away, deciding to take his words in a positive light. 'You're not so bad yourself,' she commented.

'Thank you so much for the vote of confidence,' he drawled dryly, glancing over at her. Her bright smile lit her face completely, her eyes sparkling, her perfectly pink lips wide, showing off straight white teeth. The woman really was extraordinarily beautiful. Dart cleared his throat and looked away, keeping his tone dry and impersonal. 'It means so much.'

There was no sarcasm detectable in his tone and again she thought she saw that irrepressible curve of his lips so Emmy wasn't sure whether he was joking or being serious. She'd worked alongside him, noting the way he was kind and considerate to every patient, treating each person as though they were important whether they were there for a check-up or something more serious, like a congenital heart defect. However, she had yet to figure the man out.

Not that figuring out the inner workings of Dart's mind was essential to her job here—it wasn't—but ever since she'd arrived Emmy had been intrigued by the man beside her. She couldn't quite put her finger on just why she felt that way but it was there, simmering low and deep within her.

She pushed it aside. She was here to focus on her job, on doing an important piece for the network on the plight of the Tarparnese people and those dedicated and brave people who offered help and support. That was all that mattered for the next week.

'*QaH!*' P'Ko-lat called, and Emmy recognised the Tarparniian word for 'help'. It was a word she'd heard quite often that afternoon yet it was the urgency in the receptionist's tone that made Dart stop what he was doing and rush to see what was happening.

'Look.' P'Ko-lat pointed to where two men were coming through the trees into the village clearing, carrying an injured man between them. Dart rushed over to look at his latest patient. He sucked in a breath, shook his head and then muttered directions in Tarparnese, pointing to the medical hut.

'Get me some gauze,' he called to her, as he quickly pressed his hand to the injured man's abdomen which, as they drew closer, Emmy realised was covered in blood. She did as he said and handed him the gauze as he walked past. He pressed it to the wound and yet it was soaked within less than a minute.

'Belhara, Tarvon,' he called as P'Ko-lat held open the door to the medical hut. Emmy watched as the two men ran across into the medical hut, the door closing behind them. A moment later Hunklu came out, a little dazed at being evicted from where he'd been resting. P'Ko-lat helped Hunklu as Gloria came racing over.

'What is it? What's happening?' Emmy asked, interested to find out more and annoyed she didn't speak the language.

'Emergency. Probably a gunshot wound.' Gloria disappeared inside the hut as the two men who had been carrying their friend emerged.

Gunshot. Emmy's eyes widened at this news. Guns were not her favourite thing. She knew there were soldiers, she knew the country was in a state of political unrest, but why had this man been shot? She motioned to her TV crew and together the three of them headed to the hut.

Opening the door and stepping inside, unsure of what reception she'd receive from Dart, Emmy was transfixed by the sight of Dart and Tarvon working to stabilise their patient. Gloria was cutting off the man's camouflage and Belhara was getting his equipment set up to provide anaesthesia when the time came for Dart to operate. All of them had hastily pulled on thin protective gowns over their clothes, the tapes flapping untied behind them.

She looked down at the patient, seeing the red area where the bullet had entered his body. Guns were bad, they could cause so much distress, and like a wave of sickness, Emmy felt a heaviness from her past settle over her. She closed her eyes and worked hard at controlling her emotions, staying in control. The past was the past and that's exactly where it would remain.

'If you're here to help...' Dart's deep, resonant voice broke through her control and she instantly opened her eyes, meeting his dark brown glare. 'Then grab me a bag of saline. If you're here to gawk, get out.'

Emmy looked at her crew. 'You heard the doctor. Out.' She knew they would already have shot some footage so they exited the hut without complaint. She returned her attention to Dart. 'Saline? Coming right up, Doctor.' She headed over to where she'd seen it stored earlier and passed it to him.

'Thanks.'

Taking that as a sign that her presence was acceptable, Emmy hurried to the wash basin and cleaned her hands, pulling on a gown and a pair of gloves. She was determined to be helpful whether Dart really wanted her here or not.

As the rest of the team worked, she handed Gloria the drapes and prepared the iodine so that the wound site could be sterilised before surgery. She passed Belhara the vials he couldn't quite reach and set up the operation tray for Dart.

As she tied Dart's mask in place, the patient now anaesthetised and ready for surgery, Emmy ignored the warmth radiating from his close proximity. She'd already tied Tarvon's mask in place and had felt absolutely nothing like this. Why did she only get this feeling when she was next to Dart?

Emmy swallowed over the dryness in her throat, trying not to breathe in the subtle spicy scent that surrounded him. Her fingers fumbled with the tapes, turning into a bunch of uncooked sausages as he bent down slightly, her on tiptoe, so she could reach.

He wished to goodness she'd hurry up and not because he was in any sort of pain from bending down. The sweet, fresh scent she wore, probably something extremely expensive that cost his entire year's salary, was winding its way about him, starting to infuse his senses with the need to draw her closer and breathe in more deeply.

That was the last thing he needed, to want to draw this woman closer. He'd been doing his best all day long to keep her at a firm distance but when he'd required help earlier in the clinic, he'd had to put up with her at his side. The same thing was happening now. Her help since she'd walked in the door had been great but right now he didn't need to be distracted with thoughts of what scent she was wearing when he needed to focus on removing a bullet from his patient's abdomen.

'Done. Sorry. Didn't mean to take so long.' She spoke near his ear, her breath fanning down his neck, and Dart immediately straightened, stepping closer to the table, hands held up, eyes looking down at his patient, brain processing the fact that his body was reacting to Emerson's nearness more than it had reacted to any woman in the past six years.

Dart cleared his throat as she moved away to stand next to Gloria, pleased she wasn't crowding him any more. Perhaps now he could school his thoughts to where they needed to be and not on the TV socialite who had seemingly come into this village to create havoc in any way she could. He knew that wasn't exactly true but it was certainly the way it felt.

'Belhara?' He looked at the anaesthetist.

'Ready.'

Dart held out his hand. 'Scalpel.' It was a surgery he'd performed far too many times since he'd started coming to Tarparnii. All of them knew the drill.

'Do you remove a lot of bullets?' Emmy asked into the silence.

'Yes,' Dart responded.

'Too many,' Tarvon concurred sadly.

'If we're not suturing gashes or cuts, we're delivering babies or removing bullets,' Dart continued.

Gloria nodded. 'Rick's even performed a few teeth extractions.'

Both Dart and Tarvon agreed with this.

'So, really, you become "bitsa" doctors out here. Bits of this and bits of that.'

Dart looked up and held her gaze for a moment, surprised she understood. 'Exactly. It doesn't matter what your speciality might be, whether you're a surgeon or an obstetrician, a clinic nurse or an experienced midwife. Out here, everyone does what needs to be done to the best of their ability.' Dart held out his hand. 'Forceps.'

Within a few more seconds he'd removed the bullet from the wound and Tarvon was packing it with gauze. After tidying up the area and ensuring none of the patient's vital organs had been ruptured, Dart started to close the wound in layers.

'How's he doing, Belhara?'

'Very good, Dart.'

'Excellent. Right.' Dart stood back from the patient and started to peel off his gloves. 'Must almost be time for the celebrations.'

'Celebrations?'

'Your welcome-to-the-jungle party,' Dart remarked as he finished degowning.

'I'm sorry. I'm afraid I still don't understand.' Emmy shook her head slightly as she, too, removed her gown. Dart pointed to the door and it wasn't until she'd opened the door that she realised night had fallen.

Outside, the centre of the village had undergone a transformation. Gone were the clinic tents, packed away until they were next needed. The ground had been swept with a stiff broom made of sticks, the area free of twigs and leaves. Food was being prepared, the enticing aromas filling the air, and a large bonfire was being stacked.

Everywhere people were working, busy either stringing flowers to make garlands or rolling some sort of tree sap which Emmy realised were being turned into candles. Some patients had stayed, others had returned to their own villages. She spied her own crew, taking footage of everything.

'A welcome-to-the-jungle party.' She shook her head and turned to look at Dart. 'This is all for us?'

'For you and your crew? Yes.' He'd watched her closely as she'd taken in the hub of activity before them. Where he'd thought she would expect such preferential treatment, she'd surprised him instead by appearing quite moved.

She clutched her hands to her chest and slowly exhaled. 'Never have I felt so welcomed anywhere in my life as I do here.' The words were softly spoken and Dart realised the emotions she was displaying weren't at all artificial.

She swallowed over the lump in her throat and looked at him again, her eyes brimming with tears. 'This place is…magical.'

Dart frowned and forced himself to look away from the enticing picture she made. There weren't many people who came here and saw this country, this village, these people in the same way he did, and now it appeared that Ms Emerson-Rose Jofille was one of them.

CHAPTER THREE

EMMY smothered a yawn, trying to be discreet in case anyone thought she was being rude or that she was bored. She most certainly wasn't the latter, especially as the village had held a campfire banquet in their honour. She and her crew of two, consisting of Mike, her sound man and Neal, her cameraman, had been made to feel like royalty, everyone in the village welcoming them with open arms.

Everyone, that was, except for Dart Freeman.

The man had been brisk and standoffish, especially during the past few hours since the festivities had begun. Emmy was still trying to rack her brains to figure out what she might have done wrong.

Hunklu had stayed for the campfire celebrations, continually offering her the lovely fruits and vegetables they grew in the village as well as pieces of a corn-type bread she'd seen some of the ladies making earlier.

Hunklu had been highly attentive and even though they didn't speak the same language, with a lot of gesturing they'd been able to communicate quite effectively. Dart, on the other hand, had kept his distance and even now Emmy could see him on the other side of the fire where he sat surrounded by children, talking to Jalak. The children clearly adored him and it made Emmy realise that there was something about the man that was good and proper because children were often quite good judges of character, able to pick a phoney a mile away.

'He is a quiet man,' Meeree said as she came and sat on the log next to Emmy.

'Huh? Pardon?' Emmy dragged her gaze away from the enigmatic Dart and smiled warmly at the woman beside her.

'He does what needs to be done with no fuss.'

Emmy nodded. 'A quiet achiever.' That label seemed to fit him perfectly somehow.

'You are most perceptive, Emmy. Even today he has done much for so many people.'

'He didn't go out to the other village with the rest of his medical team.' Emmy allowed her gaze to stray back to where Dart sat. 'Why not?'

Meeree smiled. 'He was the only one who could

do the clinic today on his own. He has the experience. He is also PMA leader and must be here to
meet you first.'

It was food for thought. He'd had to stay behind
because of her. Was that why he'd been standoffish? All but ignoring her? 'How many people
came to the clinic this morning?'

'Almost fifty,' Meeree supplied, and Emmy
gasped. She'd seen for herself how hectic clinics
could be.

'How...how did he finish by the time we arrived just after midday?' She now openly stared
at Dart and when he looked her way she didn't
turn away but held his gaze.

'He began well before the sun was bringing us
heat.' Meeree held out a bamboo jug in order to
refill Emmy's cup but she declined.

'Thank you but I've had too much already. You
and your people have been so generous.'

'It's their way,' a deep voice said next to her.
She turned and there, standing on the other side
of her, was Dart, a small baby, only about a month
or so old, asleep in his arms. Emmy stared up at
him, almost getting a crick in her neck he was
so tall. 'They may not have much but what they

do have they willing share with all who come to the village.'

Meeree stood and indicated that Dart should sit. 'I must check on others.'

Emmy wanted to delay Meeree, to ask her to stay so that she wasn't left alone in the glow of the campfire with the handsome but annoying Dart Freeman. Well, she had been in plenty of situations in the past where she'd had to call on her finishing-school training when faced with a situation she wasn't all that happy with.

After taking a deep breath and letting it out slowly to gain control over her body and mind, Emmy pasted a smile on her face. It didn't matter that he couldn't really see it, given the lack of bright light, she knew it was there and it was like a barrier that would protect not only her from him but him from her.

'So, please tell me, Dr Freeman, how long have you been here in the village? Meeree said that you were the senior doctor for PMA?' Emmy almost applauded herself at the way she'd managed to maintain control and open dialogue between them. If he didn't pick it up, she could sit here quietly for a few minutes and then politely move off.

'I've almost finished a twelve-week stint but I'm the PMA medic in charge in this area mainly due to the fact that I've been here so many times. I'll be returning to Australia on the same flight as you and your TV crew.' Dart didn't look at her as he spoke, instead preferring to look straight ahead.

'I'm terribly sorry that you had to wait around to welcome me and my crew this morning.'

Dart shrugged. 'Just doing my job.'

He lapsed into silence for a moment, wondering why on earth he'd come over here in the first place. He should have followed his initial instincts to keep as far away from Emerson-Rose Jofille as possible. There was something about the woman beside him, something that had called to him as he'd caught her looking his way several times that evening, but the last time…the last time she'd glanced his way, her gaze had rested on him for a long and lingering look. It was as though she'd been calling to him, beckoning him closer, and while he'd planned to resist this urge, to keep his distance, to remain highly professional where she was concerned, here he was, seated beside her, making polite small talk, something he ordinarily had no time for.

'How many years have you been coming here?'

'Six.' And if she asked him what had made him decide to come here in the first place, he would get up and walk away. He knew she was only gathering intel for her television piece, that she didn't really care what his answers were, that she was trying to find the right angle to appeal to the viewers back home. And while he acknowledged that it was her job to do that, there was no way he was going to let her poke around in his past, or his future for that matter. Emerson-Rose and her band of merry men were like mosquitoes, buzzing around and generally annoying everyone they came into contact with.

He patted the baby's bottom, shifting it slightly in his arms as the child slept on. He'd never been good at diplomatic relations but as PMA leader, he knew it was up to him to make sure that Ms Jofille's stay here was a happy one, so he had to try harder at making conversation with her.

'Uh…so what made you decide to come to Tarparnii?'

'My friend, Eden Montgomery. She's worked here in the past and told me about PMA and the great work it does. Do you know her?'

Dart's eyebrows hit his hairline. 'As a matter of fact, I do, and her husband David.' He held both colleagues in high esteem and was a little taken aback that they would be friends with someone on the rich and famous list. 'And you're friends with Eden?'

Emmy didn't miss the disbelief in his tone. 'You sound surprised, Dart. You don't think someone as wealthy and as "popular" as me has need of any friends?'

'Um…I'm sure you do. I was just surprised, that's all. Eden and David are… lovely people.'

'Implying that I'm not?' Emmy shook her head. 'Have you ever heard the cliché "Don't judge a book by its cover"?'

Now he'd gone and offended her. Dart rolled his eyes at his own stupidity. So much for being diplomatic.

She shifted to face him, ignoring the way his features where highlighted to perfection in the ambient glow of the fire. 'You know, Dart, being born into wealth, having everything you've ever wanted simply given to you, doesn't automatically make you happy. When your parents are too busy working, be it for their businesses or their philanthropic causes, to spend time with you.'

Emmy stopped. She was getting herself all worked up again and where she'd intended to be polite and diplomatic towards Dart Freeman, here she was blurting out personal information. She took another breath and continued in a calmer tone.

'I may have been given every material possession, lacking for nothing while I was growing up, but I doubt either of my parents would have sat down when I was a baby and cuddled me close, just as you're doing with this little one.'

When she was quiet he nodded, his father's words running through his mind. 'Son, when you're wrong, admit it and move on.' His father had been nothing if not a wise man. Dart cleared his throat. 'My apologies, Emerson. I had no right to be so presumptuous. I hope you can forgive me.'

It was Emmy's turn to be surprised as it wasn't every day she either received an apology or was asked for forgiveness. 'Of course I do.' She felt the fight rush out of her. 'I'm sorry, too. I didn't mean to go off on one. It's just that on most days, with the press and paparazzi, I don't usually get the opportunity to correct their misconceptions.'

Both of them were quiet for a moment, lost in

their own thoughts, absorbing the silence, and Emmy was a little surprised to find that she didn't mind so much that he'd come to sit by her side.

'What's the baby's name?' she asked after a moment, delighted with the cute little baby, if less so with the picture the pair presented. Man holding sleeping baby. It was guaranteed to melt any woman's heart.

'J'tagnan.' Even as Dart said the name, there was love in his tone and Emmy realised he had a special bond with this babe.

'What a lovely name.' Silence for a moment before she confirmed, 'Boy?'

'Yes.'

'I take it he lives in this village?'

'No.'

'Oh?'

'His mother…' Dart pointed to a woman who was cutting up more fruit and placing it onto a wooden platter '…comes from a neighbouring village. She had to walk fifty miles in order to get here to have her baby and she was in labour almost the entire time. When she stumbled into the village, the baby's head was crowning.'

'She's lucky she made it here. I've heard stories

of women giving birth either in fields or just on the side of the road. Is that really the case?'

'It's true and happens all the time.'

'J'tagnan is one of the lucky ones, then.'

'So is his mother. She had a difficult birth and has needed constant attention for the past six weeks. Tonight is really the first time she's been up and about. She's happy to be able to help out, even if it's just cutting up the fruit.'

'Will she head back to her own village soon?'

'We'll be taking her back in a few days' time.'

'You'll be going?'

He nodded. 'I need to make sure J'tagnan has everything he needs.' Dart looked down at the little babe. 'So many of them don't.'

Emmy's heart turned over at the sadness of the situation. Life here was so different from the privileged one back home in Australia and this was what she'd come here to capture. Ordinary people, living in their poverty-ridden country and all the while doing extraordinary things. 'Would you mind if we filmed J'tagnan's journey home?'

Dart's mood instantly changed with her question. Where she'd felt he was thawing a little towards her, a few simple words out of her mouth changed that entirely. His walls went back up, his entire body bristled with indignation and when he spoke, his words were more curt than before. 'These people aren't your puppets, Ms Jofille. Their lives aren't there simply so you can make compelling television.'

Emmy gritted her teeth but also realised that this was probably the reason why she'd been getting the cold shoulder from Dart. He didn't want her or her crew here at all. She'd initially thought he'd had something against her on a personal level, but perhaps it was simply that he hated all film crews. Well, it didn't matter what he thought or wanted, she was here in Tarparnii and she intended to do an amazing job on this piece so that when it aired on the network, millions and millions of people would watch, would be touched, would be galvanised into action—just as she had been when she'd first heard about the plight of the Tarparniians.

Keeping her cool and drawing on every ounce of her poise and professionalism, Emmy kept her words calm but firm. 'As I've previously mentioned, it's *Dr* Jofille, not Ms or Miss. Secondly, I have no intention of treating anyone as my puppet, Dr Freeman. Showing the good people of Australia about the situation here in Tarparnii is my key aim. I intend to ask Meeree to check with J'tagnan's mother and if the woman agrees, there's nothing you can do about it.

'Besides, I would have thought you'd be delighted that someone is aiming to shine some light on life in this little island country. We need to be educating people back home, letting them know that help is still needed, that equipment and medicines are in short supply, that people are still dying in this country from diseases that don't even exist any more in wealthy countries, such as our own, simply because we have the resources to vaccinate our children.

'What vaccinations are available to J'tagnan? What diseases can he possibly expect to be in danger of catching within the first twelve months of his life?'

Without waiting for an answer, she continued, her voice filled with her earnest enthusiasm for this cause. 'These are the things the Australian people want to know, Dr Freeman, and when they see what it's like, when they begin to understand, they will dig deep into their pockets and help provide the money to purchase those vaccinations so that J'tagnan can live a long and healthy life.

So that he can be clothed and educated and grow up to be a man who looks after his mother and is a functioning member of his country's culture.'

The words she'd spoken had come from her heart and he wondered for a moment whether he hadn't misjudged her. He allowed himself to believe that perhaps her motives for being here were honourable, that it wasn't simply about the ratings for the television network or about how doing something like this would raise her own standing in her high-society community.

Unlike so many of her peers, it seemed that Ms Jofil—no, *Dr* Jofille—intended to not only throw money at this country so she could go to sleep with a clear conscience that she'd done her part in helping put the world to rights but that she was willing to come here, to risk her life in this country of uncertainty, to show the people back in Australia and hopefully in other countries as well of the need to be doing more than they currently were.

Even in the orangey glow of the fire, Dart could see the look of determination in her eyes, could hear the vehemence in her tone, and he could make out the unyielding posture of her body. It made him wonder what it would take for her to completely lose control. Would she be as calm and as collected during a romantic interlude?

If, for example, he were to lean over and kiss her luscious mouth, how would she respond? The thought wasn't at all unappealing to him. She was, after all, an exquisitely beautiful woman, of that there was no doubt.

It was ridiculous to even allow his thoughts to wander in such a direction given that she most definitely wasn't his type at all, but as he looked at her, the colours of the night surrounding her, she looked softer yet still princess-like and perfect. A part of him wanted to see what she would look like when her calm veneer snapped.

If he were to kiss her without permission, to catch her off guard, to surprise her... Would her blue eyes flash with deep desire or utter anger? Would her mouth respond to his or would she slap his face? If she kissed him back, would she be like a wildcat, wanting more, or melt into his embrace? His mind instantly shifted into temporary overdrive as pictures of them together flashed before him, pictures of the two of them, his mouth on hers, her arms around him, their bodies close together, the heat, the need, the passion...

A loud crack from the fire snapped through

his thoughts and after blinking a few times Dart swallowed and immediately looked away from her, dropping his head to check J'tagnan, who was still asleep in his arms. He was appalled that his mind had taken such a journey, that he'd allowed himself to even think of being attracted to another woman. Even though it had been six long years since his world had erupted like a volcano, the lava spewing forth to destroy the lovely life he'd had planned, he'd never been this drawn in by another woman.

The memory of Marta, of the pure love they'd shared, had been enough to get him through… most of the time. Yet there were days and moments, such as now, when loneliness consumed him, but his mind had never consciously thought about hauling another woman close and kissing the living daylights out of her…not in the way he'd imagined holding Emerson-Rose close.

She was a woman sent here to do a job, to raise awareness of the plight of these good people, and she was offering her medical services as part of the bargain. She was a high-profile figure and combined with her medical knowledge and her engaging presence in front of the camera he had no doubt she would do a good piece, especially after the way she'd shown she really did care for these good people. Apart from that, apart from the fact that they would be spending time together over this next week, she meant nothing to him and the best thing he could do was to forget his thoughts of the past few minutes and focus on his job.

'Er…good.'

'Good?'

Dart cleared his throat, still looking at the baby, at the fire, at the people surrounding them. Looking anywhere but at her. 'It's good that you feel that way about Tarparnii. Your passion for these people…it sounds honest.'

Emmy frowned, completely confused. It had nothing to do with what Dart was presently saying but more from what had just happened. Even through the dim light around them, the glow from the fire, the atmosphere between them had thickened as Dart had looked at her as though he'd wanted to lean over and plunder her mouth. It was the oddest sensation and one that had rocked the foundations of her world.

She'd had men interested in her before and while all of them had been nice men, none had been her type. Apart from that, she'd learned never to take any man seriously given that usually they were after her wealth rather than her. Yet this man beside her obviously didn't like her and while she had no real idea why, in a strange way it was almost refreshing.

But for a moment that had changed. Perhaps the vehemence burning deep within her, the need for justice and compassion, had triggered something in the stranger sitting beside her because after she'd finished speaking, the dark look in his eyes had cleared and when his gaze had dropped— albeit momentarily—to take in the curve of her mouth, the vibe coming from him changing from one of annoyance to one of curious delight, Emmy had found herself becoming quite breathless in anticipation.

It was ridiculous. They were strangers. They knew nothing about each other and since they'd met but a few short hours ago, he'd treated her with nothing but contempt. Now, after such an intimate moment, he wasn't even looking at her. Maybe she'd imagined it. Maybe that intense look he'd given her had been just the shadows playing tricks on her mind, and as that was most defi- nitely a more likely scenario, she should forget the way Dart had made her feel all tingly and girly inside and focus on her job.

'Why...?' She stopped and cleared her throat, surprised to find it a little husky. 'Why would I lie?'

'You'd be surprised.' Dart's words were brisk. 'This isn't the first time a TV crew has come into these people's lives. It isn't the first time their hospitality has been taken advantage of. It also isn't the first time they've been duped and hurt yet they feel they need to let the crews come in the hope it will help the situation.'

'What happened?'

He shook his head. 'It was a long time ago. Over a decade. The laws governing overseas TV crews coming into this country have been changed because of the incident. It'll never happen again.'

Emmy reached out and touched his arm, only for a split second but it was enough to heighten the awareness buzzing between them. 'Tell me, please.' She clasped her hands in her lap but her tone was imploring.

Dart exhaled sharply and spoke quickly, now almost desperate to get out of her presence, to put some space between himself and the woman who was slowly starting to drive him to distraction with her close proximity.

'A crew came in, treated the villagers like their own personal slaves, getting them to do their washing, cook for them, anything and everything. They refused to walk anywhere, refused to help, and after three days of complaining about the conditions they physically wrecked five of the huts, caused injury to several of the villagers, packed up their stuff and left. Nothing was ever aired. No money came in for supplies.' He ground his teeth together. 'Worst of all, after they left, Meeree and Jalak discovered that two of the young women had been raped.'

Emmy gasped at that news. 'That's…' She couldn't talk due to the taste of utter disgust and revulsion in her mouth. She shook her head slowly. 'No wonder you're fiercely protective of these good people.' She took a swallow from the drink in her hand, wanting to wash out the foul taste. 'No one—I don't care what their circumstances are in life—*no one* should be treated that way.'

Again, the vehemence of her words surprised and pleased Dart. 'I'm glad to hear you feel that way.' Hearing her agree with him also helped ease his concern about the work Emerson-Rose and her crew were here to do.

'I'd like to assure you, Dr Freeman, that my crew and I will conduct ourselves with utter respectability. We will help out where needed and make sure Meeree and Jalak understand that we appreciate not only them but the hospitality they're providing.'

'That's good to know.' Dart was pleased by her words. It only added to the strange awareness he felt towards her and with that he knew it was time for him to move away, to put some distance between them. Kind, reassuring, enigmatic women were people he tended to avoid because they created too much havoc within him.

His fiancée Marta had been such a woman. Giving, encouraging, selfless, loving. She had been the type of woman who had always supported the underdog, who had always given far more than she'd ever received and who would fight to the nth degree for a good cause.

He found it unnerving when he came across other women of such high integrity and where he'd thought Emerson-Rose to be a pampered little princess, playing at a game of public relations, he was starting to discover that there were a few more layers to her than he'd previously thought.

He was definitely intrigued…and that spelled danger!

CHAPTER FOUR

EMMY watched as Dart stood and without another word walked away, back to where the baby's
mother was busy still cutting up fruit, the young
village children crowding around her and waiting
for a piece of fresh… Emmy wasn't sure what
type of fruit it actually was, tasting between a
pear and banana. Either way it was delicious as
well as refreshing, which was why the children
all wanted more.

The mother was getting tired, standing up, doing
the manual work, especially if her body was still
recovering from a traumatic birth. Dart manoeuvred his way through the gaggle of children and
with a gentle hand urged the mother away, sitting
her down before handing her sleeping baby over.
The woman smiled at him with gratitude, which
he accepted with a simple nod of his head before
turning to finish cutting up the fruit and giving
it out to the children.

'He is a man who always gives.' Meeree had sat down quietly beside Emmy, startling her.

'Huh? Sorry?' She quickly tore her gaze away from the man who seemed able to captivate her thoughts.

'Dartagnan.' Meeree gestured in Dart's direction.

Emmy was confused for a split second longer then her eyes widened in surprise. 'That's his name? Dartagnan? I didn't realise.' She paused then said his name again. 'Dartagnan.' She allowed the sound of his name to roll around in her mouth, teasing her tongue. She liked it. It was a strong, brave name and it suited him perfectly. Another thought popped into her mind. 'Wait. The baby is called J'tagnan.'

Meeree nodded, her kind wise face highlighted in the glow from the fire. 'He delivered the babe. Rescued the babe. Made it breathe again. The mother was filled with gratitude. She mixed the name of my *par machkai*, Jalak, with that of her rescuer and protector of her first child, Dartagnan. Jalak means protector and Dartagnan means leader. J'tagnan will grow to be a strong man for his village.'

'Leader.' Emmy spoke the word softly and

couldn't help the smile that touched her lips as she turned to once more look at Dart. He had finished his job of handing out fruit and was now crouched down beside J'tagnan's mother, making sure she was feeling all right. 'He's quite a man, isn't he, Meeree?'

'Yes, he is. Our village is more rich when he is here. He gives to all. It doesn't matter if people are high up in their village or not. He gives to all but, Emmy…' There was a hint of sadness in Meeree's tone. 'Dartagnan has no one to give to *him*.'

'You care about him more than the other PMA staff, yes?'

Meeree's smile was calm and natural. 'People come for many reasons. Some to help, some to seek, some for solace. It is the ones who come for solace who need the most love.'

'Dart needs solace?' Emmy was surprised at that.

Meeree stretched out a hand and lightly touched Emmy's cheek. 'He is not the only one. You have much in common.'

Emmy held the woman's gaze, unsure for a brief moment what she meant. She didn't have long to wait as Meeree continued.

'I see you look at him across the fire. You feel him. You do not know why. He is like someone you once knew from a dream but on waking, you have forgotten.'

To say Emmy was completely stunned by the other woman's words was an understatement. It was true. Even though Dart had been a touch brash and a bit standoffish since they'd met earlier that day, Emmy hadn't been able to shake the connection she felt with him. She couldn't explain it, she couldn't describe it, but it was just as Meeree had said. It was like she knew Dart but from a dream where life was all fuzzy and mixed up.

'How can you know that?' Emmy was quietly stunned. She was by no means disputing the words the wise woman spoke.

Meeree shrugged her shoulders with natural modesty. 'I have insights.'

'Like a psychic?'

'No. I look at people and I *see* them.' She waved her hands as though it really wasn't relevant. 'You have a space in your heart filled with loneliness. Everything you have been given does not fill this emptiness.'

'It's so true,' Emmy breathed.

Meeree pointed to where Dart now stood, talking to Jalak and a few of the other men in the village. He was standing in profile so she couldn't quite make out his features but the vision of the tall, handsome man shrouded in shadows from the night was just like the man who had come to her in her dreams.

Of course, she'd been dreaming of a tall, dark and handsome stranger since she'd been about twelve, a man who had good morals and ethics, a man who put others first, a man who would look into her eyes, see into her soul and love her for who she was deep down inside. That man from her dreams, her knight in shining armour, had always been a bit faceless...until now.

Over the years, as she'd grown wise to the ways of the world, as she'd tried one relationship after another only to find that their main motive was her extensive family fortune, Emmy had started to become cynical, doubting she'd ever find her Mr Right.

'Dart has such a space, an emptiness, like yours. A void. He is filled with loneliness. It is why he gives. Giving helps to cover up the hole in his heart, but it does not heal it.'

Emmy nodded slowly, her throat dry and

constricting slightly with Meeree's soft words. Dart was lonely. Just like her. Apparently they had something in common after all. They could fill their worlds with people, with experiences that made them feel less alone, but at the end of the day it was just them and their void, trying to sleep, telling themselves that tomorrow was another day where they could once more do good work in order to try and keep the dark hunger of sadness from consuming them.

She took a sip from her drink, swallowing over the lump in her larynx, taking in a healing breath and nodding. 'Thank you.' She wasn't exactly sure what she was thanking Meeree for but it didn't seem to matter. The world, her life back in Australia, the ebbs and flows of her parents' constant nagging for her to take her rightful place in society, the need to do more than just throw money at the poor—everything seemed to pale in comparison to knowing there was someone else out there, feeling the same as her.

That light spark of knowledge helped Emmy to feel less alone than she'd felt in years. Even though she had no idea what had caused Dart's loneliness, at the moment it didn't matter.

'I was given everything I ever wanted when

I was growing up,' she said quietly to Meeree. 'My parents are very wealthy,' she added as clarification. 'Yet they were so busy giving charity to others that they seemed to forget about my brother and I.'

'Money can bring so much happiness but only when it is used with wisdom. Your brother? He is older?'

Emmy's smile was natural as she thought of Tristan. 'He is. He was very wild as a teenager and about ten years ago he ended up in hospital after a bad car accident. It took him over a year to recover properly but it changed him.'

'He is happy?'

She sighed. 'He tells me he is but...' She shook her head. 'I don't know. I think he is. He is in charge of one of my father's businesses. The accident helped him to find a clear direction, just as medicine helped me to find a direction.'

'I feel, maybe, that this direction was not what you hoped it would be. It did not give you the peace you still seek.'

Emmy laughed without humour. 'You are extremely perceptive, Meeree. When my parents realised I was serious about studying medicine, they donated a lot of money to the hospital where

I was doing my training. There's even a building named after my family—the Jofille Wing.'

'This brought you special treatment you did not want.'

'Exactly. I insisted my professors treat me like every other student, that they grade me accordingly.'

'Did they?'

She shrugged and spread her hands wide. 'I don't know. I achieved high marks in most of my subjects, I'd been treated fairly during my intern rotations and then I had one job after the next handed to me on a silver platter.'

'And yet you wonder if you are a good doctor?'

'Yes. Yes, I do. All these years later and I'm still questioning myself. Did the hospitals I worked at keep me happy so my parents would continue to donate money? Did I earn my grades or was I awarded them simply because I was a Jofille?'

'Is the answer important?'

Emmy frowned as she considered Meeree's question. 'Well, I like helping people. I was taught very early in my life the benefits of public relations and when I was offered the job at the television station—which my father setup for me in an effort to get me to do more "public profile" work—I thought it might give me the opportunity to combine these areas.'

'So you came here.'

'Yes. I can use my connections and PR skills as well as help out in a medical capacity. My crew and I have already done a few television pieces on doctors who work in the Australian outback, showing the incredible work they do, showing the viewers the unsung heroes, highlighting topics that have been ignored for far too long.'

Meeree patted her hand. 'Doubt has no meaning when you know you are doing good work.'

Emmy thought back over her day, how when Hunklu had come into the village, his hand bleeding from the gash, Dart hadn't wanted her help. It had hurt to be turned away but in the end she'd been able to give Hunklu the after-treatment care he deserved and even though she didn't speak Tarparnese, she knew how to offer compassion.

When the clinic had started, she'd again felt doubt as to what she was meant to do, until Dart had needed her assistance. Even though she hadn't had an official role, it had still been great to help out. She'd been trained as a GP with a fair knowledge of emergency medicine but working at a

TV network didn't give her much opportunity to practise medicine.

Doubt has no meaning when you know you are doing good work. Meeree's words floated around in her head and filled her heart with hope.

Perhaps Tarparnii might do more to help her than she could do to help it. If she could discover the answers to her questions, to continue to move forward to find out more about herself, then surely everything would be worth it. Her loneliness had been with her for as long as she could remember, sparking to life when she'd been kidnap— No. She wouldn't think about that. Not now.

'Dart. Dart.' Emmy looked to where some of the young children were running towards him, wide grins on their faces. 'Puppets,' they called, their words sounding strangely guttural as they spoke in English. 'Puppets, please.'

Emmy turned to Meeree to ask what the children meant but found the woman had left her side as quietly as she'd arrived. She looked around and spotted Meeree coming out of a hut with a large white sheet. Jalak and the rest of the men were collecting long sticks from the ground and right before her very eyes the sheet was erected like a screen.

'Puppets?' she asked herself softly, and stood to go closer, to find out what was going on. Everyone else was gathering around, wide beaming smiles on their faces. Emmy was transfixed by what was happening and within a few minutes Dart took his place behind the sheet, the firelight coming from behind him making shadows on the white sheet.

In wonderment, she watched as two hands formed the shape of an eagle, coming down to settle at the lower part of the sheet. The eagle fluttered his wings and then a soft, ethereal sound came from Meeree, who was standing near. She lifted her voice in sweet song, not singing any words but a lilting melody of pure beauty as Dart continued to contort his hands into different shapes, animals, flowers, trees and sometimes humans walking along.

The children were quiet, watching intently. In fact, everyone was quiet as they sat, spellbound by the wonderful skill Dart was exhibiting. Meeree had already mentioned that they didn't usually have big bonfires unless it was a special occasion and tonight the occasion had been a small gathering to welcome her and her crew. That meant that the shadow puppets were a rare treat and something Dart was extremely good at. No wonder the children had begged him for this treat. Emmy was mesmerised.

Those hands. Those clever, clever hands. They worked quickly and effectively to help and heal people, they lovingly cradled a baby, they created enjoyment for everyone... And Emmy couldn't help but wonder what it would feel like to have those clever hands holding hers, touching her arms, her body, threading those long fingers into her hair.

She'd never realised how clever a man's hands could be before but knowing he could do so much with them, she wanted to know more. As he changed his hands to make another animal, Emmy sidled around to the rear of the sheet, ensuring she kept well away from the light he was using, and simply stood there watching him. From this angle, the way he contorted his hands just looked like gnarled knuckles and fingers intertwined in a big old mess yet the opposite side had revealed a perfect picture.

Wasn't that how her life seemed sometimes? All gnarled knuckles on the inside but shining brightly on the outside? She wished her life was different. That she felt shiny on the inside as well as the outside. Hopefully here, in this world that seemed to be completely different from everything she'd ever experienced, she would find her inner shininess.

As Dart brought his show to a close, Meeree's voice trailing off, the round of applause they received caused goose-bumps to spread over her body. Emmy was so overcome she was unable to clap. She just stood there, a little behind him and to the left and watched as he stood, took Meeree's hand in his and took a bow.

He brought Meeree's hand to his lips in a kiss of thanks before turning—and that's when he saw her. They were surrounded by firelight, nothing between them except for the hazy smoke-filled air. It added to the effect of seeing her there, standing still, watching him intently. Her trim figure was outlined perfectly, her hair still hanging down her back in a long plait, but the loose tendrils, the way the breeze teased at them…she looked glorious. Such beauty.

No doubt she knew full well the effect she had on the male species but he seriously didn't want to be one of those captured in her net.

Meeree and Jalak were folding up the sheet, Meeree shoving him gently out of the way in

Emerson-Rose's direction. Dart found himself looking down at her, the fire, already dying down, not too far away from them. Was the intense heat that surrounded him from the fire or from Emmy?

If he took one more step, he'd be almost toe to toe with her, stepping into her comfort zone, allowing her to break into his. Personal space. Personal barriers. He'd erected them a long time ago and that stopped him now from following through on the urge to draw closer to her. Like a moth to the flame, he thought, and shook his head with a hint of self-derision.

'You didn't enjoy the show?' He broke the silence, not wanting to dwell on the way he'd thought she'd been looking at him. The irises of her eyes were almost completely covered by her pupils, giving her that wide-eyed innocent look that seemed to be drawing him in, begging him to come hither. The woman was creating a sense of uneasiness within him and he most certainly didn't appreciate it.

'Uh…on the contrary. You're…' Emmy swallowed and smiled brightly at him, her eyes wide with wonder '…amazing. I've never seen anyone do shadow puppets before. That's quite a gift.'

Her tone was almost bursting with appreciation and Dart had to work hard not to be affected by her praise. He'd done shows before and been thanked before, people surprised at this strange skill he had, and, besides, it was only in places like this that he played around with making shadow puppets. So why was it that Emmy's words made him feel all chuffed and happy inside? He hardly knew the woman yet her words, for some strange reason, meant so much.

'Where did you learn to do that?'

'My father taught me.'

She smiled and nodded. 'That's wonderful.'

Dart shrugged. 'We didn't own a television when I was young and it passed the time.'

'You didn't own a television?' The words were out of her mouth before she could stop them.

'I'll bet you were raised in a house that had a television in every room.' There was bitterness to his words and Emmy felt her hackles begin to rise.

'Don't go presuming you know anything about me, Dart Freeman,' she said softly. Her tone was still controlled but her hands had gone from being relaxed at her sides into firm fists. 'I would have gladly traded in every television in my home in order to spend some one-on-one time with my father. In fact, I'd have traded in everything I owned.'

And that most certainly put him in his place. 'You're right, Emerson. I humbly apologise once more.'

They stood there for a moment longer, just staring at each other, before Dart inclined his head slightly in a bow of respect, then turned to help pack things away. Space, he needed space and distance from the woman who was starting to rile him faster than a child hitting a hornet's nest with a stick. As he turned, he noticed the camera crew, equipment out, filming what was going on.

He'd temporarily forgotten about them and as he moved, he realised they were trailing their equipment after *him*. Anger bubbled inside him. They were here to film the villagers, not him. They were supposed to be highlighting the poverty in the area, the needs of this isolated community, not focusing on the lonely doctor who came to this small country, a country that was in the grips of civil unrest, in order to help out and not feel so lonely any more.

Making a scene was not his style. Ordering them to turn off the cameras was not his style.

He'd speak to Emerson tomorrow about how they most certainly did not have his permission to include anything about him in their little documentary. Right now, though, as he continued to help pack things away, checking with Tarvon who had been monitoring Weyakuu, the gunshot victim, as well as ensuring J'tagnan and his mother were settled for the night, Dart prepared to turn in.

He was pleased to be sleeping in one of the huts that was already full of PMA personnel as it meant that Emerson-Rose and her crew would be sleeping in another. It meant he could put the socialite out of his mind. She may have shown some hidden depth, she may have proven herself to be adept at assisting in medical procedures, but she would always be part of the rich and famous set while he was definitely from the other end of the social spectrum.

Same planet, different worlds.

The next morning, he was woken by the sounds of tinkling laughter and as he pulled on some clothes, stepping over Rick and Gloria who were still sleeping, Dart headed outside to greet the new day.

Thoughts of a blue eyed beauty with long

flowing auburn hair had flooded his dreams, causing him to wake frequently, thoughts of what it might be like to press his lips to hers, wondering if she'd taste as good as she looked. He wasn't usually a man who was attracted to the outside package but he had to admit that Emerson-Rose was easily one of the most stunningly beautiful women he'd ever seen. Therefore, he'd rationalised, it was only natural that he might be attracted to such a woman—as was every other man.

Somewhere around two o'clock, he'd given up on sleeping and insisted on relieving Tarvon for a few hours. Monitoring a patient was far better than tossing and turning and being unable to control his thoughts. By the time Tarvon returned, just before six o'clock, Weyakku was stable and improving nicely. Dart had returned to the hut, intending to rest his eyes for half an hour, but had obviously fallen asleep as the time was now just after eight.

The sound of the laughter came again and he knew instinctively that it was hers—Emerson's. He headed to the food hut and found her seated next to Belhara, smiling brightly, her eyes sparkling with laughter and delight at whatever it was the anaesthetist had just said.

Jalak, Hunklu and Sue were also in the food hut, everyone wearing smiles. Emerson's TV crew was sitting and eating and where Dart was usually up before the sun, he found that he felt a little odd and a bit left out, walking into the hut so late.

'Hello sleepyhead,' Sue said in the form of a greeting. 'I hear Weyakuu is improving?'

'Have you checked with Tarvon this morning?' he asked Sue.

Sue stood from her seat, next to Emerson-Rose, and carried her plate to the wash basin. 'I looked in earlier. I'm just on my way to relieve him. Take a seat.' Sue indicated the spot she'd just vacated. 'Eat.'

Dart smiled politely and realised there were no other vacant seats in the hut except for the one next to Emerson. It would be churlish to refuse to sit so close to the woman who had filled his night with such vivid thoughts.

Careful to avoid unnecessary contact, Dart manoeuvred himself onto the long bench seat between Emerson and Mike. Belhara offered him a plate of fruit, which he gratefully accepted. Dart ignored the way her sweet scent wound around him and he most definitely ignored the way the brief touch of her smooth legs against his hairy ones ignited the dying embers of the dreams he was trying to forget.

He just needed to act as if this was any other day, focus his thoughts on eating and at the first opportunity excuse himself. Thankfully, though, the conversation resumed and as he ate, Dart learned the reason why he'd woken to Emerson's laughter. Belhara had been regaling her with stories from his boyhood when he'd often swing on vines into the waterhole that wasn't too far from here.

'I'd love to see it. We should definitely get some footage of such a place,' Emmy said, desperately trying not to notice the warmth radiating from Dart as he sat close beside her. She could have cheerfully kicked Sue when the woman had offered Dart her seat. Emmy hadn't slept very well last night yet it had had nothing to do with being in a different country, or the fact that this was her first overseas piece for the network.

Her lack of sleep could be put down to one particular person—Dartagnan Freeman.

Obviously her subconscious had been listening to her body, the two of them in cahoots regarding

the attraction she felt for the tall, brooding surgeon. Her body had responded instantly to his
closeness. His thigh almost pressing against hers
and the fact that they both wore shorts, due to the
early morning heat, meant that if she shifted even
marginally, her naked leg would brush against
his again, causing complete havoc within her
body.

'The waterhole, it is not far.' Jalak was inform-
ing her, yet Emmy was having difficulty concen-
trating on his words, her mind electrified with
the mild spicy scent she equated with Dart. 'A
journey there would be of great benefit on such
an early morning of sunshine.'

'Where are we journeying to now?' Tarvon said
as he came into the hut.

'Waterhole,' Belhara said.

'Excellent. Let me eat then we'll definitely
head there.' He put a hand on Dart's shoulder
and squeezed himself in between Dart and Mike,
all but squashing Dart into Emerson.

'Sorry,' Dart muttered close to her ear, his tone
deep and husky as his arm brushed accidentally
across her breast. The touch burned into his skin,
her breathing hot on his cheek as she tried not to
look too embarrassed by the nearness they'd been

forced into. Dart braced his arm on the table, holding himself as upright as he could, the muscles flexing as he closed his eyes and waited for Tarvon to stop moving. Good heavens she smelled good. Good enough to eat.

'Pardon?' Emmy breathed, her mouth now close to his ear.

Dart eased back, Tarvon now settled. 'Nothing.' Had he thought out loud? Mortification ripped through him and he made sure he didn't meet her gaze, focusing on eating so he could get away from her close proximity.

When Mike and Neal stood, making more room on the bench, Dart thought he heard Emerson breathe a sigh of relief and within a split second of there being more room, he'd all but shoved Tarvon down to the other end of the bench, thankful for some much-needed space.

'I'd better go and change,' he heard her mumble, and a moment later she'd scrambled to her feet and had disappeared from the food hut. He closed his eyes and concentrated on returning his breathing, his thoughts and his over-sensitised body to normal.

'You all right, Dart?' Tarvon asked.

Dart opened his eyes and looked at his friend, shrugging slightly. 'Your guess is as good as mine.'

CHAPTER FIVE

WITHIN half an hour, a group of them were all ready to traipse to the waterhole, Dart making sure he kept quite a bit of distance between himself and Emerson-Rose.

Tarvon and Belhara, who both seemed to be besotted by the socialite, led the way, a tired Rick and Gloria talked to the TV crew, pointing out different sights that they felt should be included in the Tarparnii footage.

'This country is so incredibly beautiful,' he could hear Gloria saying, and Emerson turned around to agree. 'I mean, just look at this.' Gloria stopped walking and pointed out a tree that had three trunks. 'It was split open by lightning, and look here.' The nurse all but dragged Emerson over. 'New life grew right out of the middle of the old tree that was split in half. Three trunks.'

Dart walked past the little group, continuing on his way.

'Don't you want to stop and look at the tree?'

Emerson asked, and he looked over his shoulder, not realising she'd caught up with him.

'I've seen it plenty of times. Quite remarkable.' Polite and distant. That was his plan and he would succeed just so long as he ignored her intoxicating scent, her gorgeous body—now clad in a one-piece swimsuit with a sarong tied around her waist—and her efforts at small talk.

'Yes, it is.' They trudged on for another minute or two, swatting away insects that were also enjoying the heat. Emmy racked her mind for something to talk about and knew that the weather was always the safest topic given that it affected everyone in one way or another.

'Do you think it will rain today?'

'Yes.'

Emmy tried not to huff, keeping her impatience with him in check. 'I understand that Weyakuu is progressing nicely.'

'Correct.'

She paused. 'When do you think Hunklu will be well enough to return home?'

'Soon.'

Emmy threw her arms out wide. 'What is it with you?' she demanded, frustration getting the better of her.

'Sorry?' He raised a quizzical eyebrow but kept walking. They were almost there. Almost at the waterhole.

'I'm trying to make conversation, trying to engage in a bit of a discussion as we walk along, and yet I'm left with the distinct impression that you don't like me.'

'Really?'

'There you go again. Mr one-word-answer man. First you're distant, then you're polite, then, when you do talk to me, you usually insult me, then you apologise and walk away.' She frowned, wondering if she shouldn't just shut up and ignore him as much as he was her, but she also knew it simply wasn't in her nature. She was a people person and yet the one person she was really interested in talking to, not only because, as Meeree had pointed out last night, there seemed to be some strange sort of connection between herself and Dart but also because she'd caught glimpses of the man beneath the surface he presented to her. It was *that* man she wanted to get to know.

'You are baffling, Dartagnan Freeman.'

'Baffling?' The more she talked, the more he was finding it difficult not to engage with her. They were almost there. Tarvon and Belhara had already disappeared in front of them, meaning they'd turned the final corner. Emerson's nearness, her obvious frustration and confusion were highly enticing as her brow puckered into a small frown, her blue eyes registering her emotions, her plump pink lips parted as she sighed again with frustration.

He wasn't used to people simply speaking their minds, especially when it had to do with emotions, and for a second he wasn't sure whether to drop an arm about her shoulders and pull her close in order to reassure her that he did indeed want to talk to her or whether to increase his stride and walk off, leaving her to draw from his actions what she would.

'Yes, baffling. You keep your distance from me wherever possible but on another level I sense that all you really want to do is sit quietly somewhere and talk to me.'

'Hmm.' Dart was surprised at her astuteness. It seemed to be that the attraction he felt for her wasn't one-sided and that should be enough of a reason for him to keep his distance. They rounded the corner and all they needed to do was to climb over the rocks that surrounded the waterhole and they'd be there.

'After you.' He held out his hand to indicate she should go first.

'Ha. You do realise that was two words,' Emmy teased as she started to scramble over the rocks. The stones were smooth in places where people often walked and it wasn't at all difficult to traverse. She was wearing flip-flops on her feet and carrying a rolled-up towel beneath her arm. 'I mean, I wouldn't want you to knock yourself out by actually having a conversation with me,' she continued, still in a bit of a mood. 'After all, I'm part of the annoying television crew here to disrupt the last week of your rotation.'

She continued talking as they clambered over the rocks, Dart going behind her, trying not to notice the flash of her gorgeous legs peeking out between the folds of the colourful sarong as she moved.

'And then,' she said, 'just when I think I have you all figured out, you hold a baby in your arms or make incredible shadow pup—*Arrgh*.' Emmy's foot slipped on one of the rocks and she overbalanced, falling backwards into Dart's firm chest, his arms coming securely around her body.

Both of them stilled and time froze around them as they seemed to lean more heavily against each other. The sweet softness of her supple body was so close to his, her enticing scent filling his senses, making him exhale slowly and deeply as he tried desperately to ignore the way her silky hair brushed against his T-shirt-covered chest. Good heavens, the woman felt exquisite so close to him.

His breath rushed past her ear, causing goose-bumps to spread down her bare arms, coolness combining with the warmth flooding through her at his firm touch. Emmy knew she had to shift, knew she had to right herself, but couldn't help savouring the way it felt to have Dart's arms about her, the warmth of his chest pressing into her neck and shoulders.

Carefully, and without a word, his hands slipped to her waist as he shifted her to stand upright. 'Are you OK?' His rich, deep tone washed over her and Emmy parted her lips, desperate to get her erratic breathing under control before this man could see just how much his touch was affecting her. 'Emerson?'

'Fine.'

'Are you sure? You didn't twist your ankle?' Medical. If he focused on the medical side, ensuring she was indeed all right, perhaps he'd be able to push aside just how incredible it had felt to have her in his arms. His hands were still at her waist, waiting for her to put full weight onto her left foot. 'Emerson?'

Clearing her throat and forcing herself to pay attention to the signals her brain was busy sending out, Emmy pushed aside the fog that had clouded her brain at his touch. 'Good.' She shifted completely out of his arms and turned to glance up at him. 'See? Fine.'

He raised a teasing eyebrow. 'Now who's monosyllabic?'

Emmy gave him a tight smile but returned her full attention to getting over the rest of the rocks, and within a moment she could see Belhara and Tarvon about ready to dive into the water, their towels left higher up on one of the rocks. Trees accompanied the rocks around a natural spring-fed body of water, spread out for them to enjoy.

'What took you so long?' Tarvon asked as Belhara dived in.

'Sorry,' Emmy responded, and shifted further away from Dart. She needed distance from him because at the moment she was still coming to terms with how incredible it had felt to be held so close, so near to the man who had plagued her dreams all night long. There was a definite attraction between the two of them and with the way he'd breathed her scent in, his hands having caressed her waist before he'd eventually let her go, Emmy knew distance was a good idea.

'Come on in. The water is great,' Belhara called.

'OK.' Emmy ditched her towel, took off her flip-flops and the sarong and pulled her hair free of the band, the soft, silky tresses finally let loose.

Dart sucked in a breath as he watched her graceful movements and moments later as she dived beneath the cool, refreshing water, surfacing near Tarvon and Belhara, the three of them laughing, he experienced the strangest sensation of anger. He clenched his jaw and curled his hands into fists as he watched her enjoying herself with his friends. He hadn't felt this way in an incredibly long time and it took him a while to realise that perhaps it wasn't anger he was experiencing but rather something much, much worse.

Jealousy.

Unfortunately for Dart's peace of mind, there was no clinic that morning. He was in the mood to lose himself in medicine, to concentrate on procedure, to do what needed to be done. However, all that needed to be done at the moment was to have some downtime after the last few hectic days.

He should relax and read a book but every time he tried to turn his mind to the story before him he would hear Emerson laugh, or she'd make a comment, or he'd hear her giving directions to her crew. Hadn't they shot enough footage by now? Surely they didn't need to stay until the end of the week and could leave sooner.

He spent time monitoring Weyakuu, giving the others the opportunity to pander to their inner peacock and spend time in front of the camera or being interviewed by Emerson. When a call came through on the UHF radio requesting medical assistance be sent to the village where Hunklu lived, Dart was thankful to be doing something at last. He'd already checked Hunklu's sutures and rebandaged the man's hand so he was cleared to head back to his village.

Dart was in the process of gathering supplies together when Tarvon and Emerson came into the storage hut. 'Call come in?' Tarvon asked.

'Yes. Nothing urgent. Medical assistance is required at Hunklu's village. It's not too far away so I thought I'd take Rick and Gloria and head off. Might be an overnighter but I'll be back to-morrow morning, ready to transfer J'tagnan and his mother.' He tried not to look at Tarvon and Emerson, keeping his focus on his work, getting supplies packed. He had no idea why he should feel animosity towards Tarvon simply because he was standing beside Emerson, had been talking to Emerson, had been making Emerson laugh. She meant nothing to him.

'You can't go, Dart.'

'What?' Dart straightened and looked at his friend.

'This is my testing week,' Tarvon interjected. 'I'm supposed to be point man on any emergencies, organising the teams and supplies.' He grinned and shook his head. 'You're just so used to being in charge.' He turned to look at Emmy. 'Our Dart is a natural-born leader.'

'So I've been told.' Emmy was carefully watching the interchange between the two men. They were almost like two brothers, the younger begging for the chance to prove himself.

'Of course you're right, Tarvon.' Dart straightened, shoved his hands into the pockets of his shorts and stepped back from the equipment. 'The call is that two pregnant women are experiencing strong contractions.'

'Double birth.' Tarvon nodded and Emmy could see the young doctor's mind whirring quickly into action. 'I'll take Belhara and Bel with me. Rick and Gloria have been angling for some "quality" time together so chances are they'll kick you out of the hut tonight.' Tarvon grinned at his friend.

Emmy looked quickly at Dart. 'Does that mean you'll need to stay in the hut I was in last night?'

'Yes.'

'Oh.' She bit her lip and a slight tinge coloured her cheeks, Dart wasn't sure why. 'Can I go with you, Tarvon? Bring my crew to film the—'

'Sorry, no can do,' Tarvon interjected. 'The Tarparniians are very private with their birthing practices. Family only. They won't be appreciative of outsiders.'

She turned to face Dart. 'Well…looks as though you *are* going to be stuck with me.'

Dart forced a smile, being polite. It seemed to be the name of the game between the two of them, especially since the waterhole incident where her body had been pressed firmly against his. 'Great.' The word was said between clenched teeth, his lips pulled tight. For the first time he was grateful for the presence of her crew. At least they would be in the same hut all night long.

After dinner, a much quieter affair than the festivities of the previous night, Dart collected his bedroll from the hut, Rick and Gloria thanking him for allowing them some time alone. Emerson was talking with her crew, who were standing by one of the transport trucks with their camera and sound equipment.

When he entered the second sleeping hut, with its bamboo walls and thatched roof, which would provide more than adequate cover from any rain that might fall during the night, Dart couldn't believe how exhausted he felt. It had been a hectic few days and it was all starting to catch up with him.

As he readied for bed, brushing his teeth, rolling out his mat and setting up the blankets and pillows, he allowed himself to reflect that any wayward thoughts he had towards Ms Jofille were ludicrous and very temporary. She would walk in and out of his life, having no impact whatsoever before returning to her own privileged lifestyle, telling people to support the efforts of PMA by sending money to provide further medical care.

He reflected on the time he'd spent with her so far, and in one respect he didn't seem to know anything about her, yet in another it was as though he'd known her for much longer. He *had* been impressed when she'd spoken about her current project from the heart just as he'd also felt a pang of sorrow when she'd confessed to never getting to spend time with her father. He'd had ample proof both in his own life in Australia and here on Tarparnii to know that happiness couldn't be bought, and that slight glimpse she'd allowed him into her life had made him ponder just what else she'd missed out on due to the wealth and circumstances she'd been born into.

He was lying on his mat, hands laced behind his head as he stared up at the thatched roof, determined to remove thoughts of Emmy from his mind, when the door to the hut opened. Dart closed his eyes for a moment, not wanting to deal with a medical emergency at this time but knowing it was his job to do so. At least he was already dressed, having learned very early on during his first visit to Tarparnii that it was much easier to sleep in light trousers, his torch next to his pillow, his shoes always ready at the door.

'What's the problem?' he asked as he sat up and opened his eyes. He was in the process of reaching for his torch when he realised the intrusion wasn't about a medical emergency. Although she stood in silhouette, he didn't need to have a light on to know Emerson-Rose had entered the hut, her sweet fresh scent winding its way about him.

'Er...there's no problem.' She walked carefully over to where her bedroll and her backpack were situated.

'What...what are you doing?' He sat up straighter, his mind working frantically, already knowing exactly what she was doing and why but rejecting it at the same time.

'Getting ready to sleep.'

'Right. Uh...Emerson?'

'Yes.'

'Where are your crew? Are they coming soon?'

'Nope.'

'Nope? What do you mean, "nope"?'

'They're heading out with Jalak and a few

of the men on an all-nighter to get some night footage.'

'But it's not safe. There are soldiers with guns out there…at night. It's just not safe.' Neither was it safe for him in here, alone with Emmy. He wanted those men in here now. Otherwise it would mean that he and Emmy would be alone *all night long* in the hut. Alone. Sue was monitoring the patient tonight and Dart had been relying on the fact that Emmy's crew would be here.

'That's what I said but both Jalak and Meeree have told me my crew will be fine. They did, however, say it was no place for me and so I've basically been "sent to bed", as it were.' She tried to laugh, to lighten the strained atmosphere as she unrolled her sleeping mat. It contained a mat filled with down, a sheet and a pillow.

Dart shook his head. This wasn't happening. 'I can sleep somewhere else, if you prefer,' he remarked, trying to be diplomatic as well as ignoring the deep, almost sensual nature of his tone. The thought of himself and Emmy alone in the hut all night long… 'I'll go sleep in the medical tent. That way, if an emergency comes in, you don't need to worry about your sleep being disturbed.'

Something in his words, his tone made her bristle. Didn't the man want her help? Didn't he think she was a serious doctor? That obtaining a medical degree had just been something she'd undertaken so she didn't get bored? She shook her head and knelt on the mat, her fingers working quickly as she pulled the band from her hair and undid the plait.

'First and foremost, Dartagnan, I'm registered with PMA to provide medical care during my stay. If there is a medical emergency tonight, I'm more than capable of assisting in whatever capacity you require.' She reached into the side of her pack where she kept her torch, hoping she'd made her point and pleased she'd kept her voice firm yet in control. Hopefully now Dartagnan Freeman would get the message that she was here to help.

'Now, if you don't mind, I need to turn the torch on to look through my backpack.' Without waiting for his reply, she pressed the button and light illuminated the entire hut instantly. She glanced over at Dart…and stared.

He was sitting up on his mat, his firm, muscled torso bare to the waist. Her mouth went instantly dry at the sight, her heart rate increasing, her eyes wide as she looked him over.

She knelt there, torch in hand, her gaze warm on his body, but all Dart's sluggish mind could register was how utterly amazing she looked, her long auburn locks framing her face and shoulders. The torch light provided a magnificent glow, a halo of light shining above her head, and his mouth went instantly dry at the sight, his heart rate increasing, his eyes dreamy as he looked at her.

'Emmy.' He breathed her name as though she were the most precious thing in the world. 'You're stunning!'

CHAPTER SIX

THE world around them seemed to stop while the atmosphere in the room thickened with growing awareness. Emmy couldn't believe what he'd just said. Had he said it? Had she imagined it? She couldn't recall the last time a man had looked at her so openly, his eyes glazed with passion and desire.

She tried to swallow over the tingling in her throat, the tingling that seemed to be spreading throughout her entire body as their eyes continued to hold, as her awareness of him grew, as the need for one of them to break this silence increased. If not, things might really start to get out of control.

Never had she felt such an instant attraction to a man before yet here she was, kneeling, torch in hand, light glowing around the room, making it even more cosy, more personal, more intimate.

'Did...?' She stopped and cleared her throat. 'Did you just say...?' She couldn't do it. The astonishment in her voice was evident that she couldn't believe he'd really said what he had. He thought she was stunning? Really?

Dart closed his eyes, blocking the sight of her from burning itself into his mind but realised he was already too late. She was…breathtaking, kneeling there, looking at him in disbelief at what he'd just said. How could he have been so stupid?

'Uh…I didn't mean to say that out loud.'

Emmy paused for a beat, still trying to compute everything. 'But you do *think* I'm…' She couldn't even bring herself to repeat such a wonderful compliment in case she woke herself up from this strange but very pleasing dream. While she'd lived most of her life as a public figure, both in Australia and to a lesser extent overseas, Emmy had *never* believed anything ever written about her. In fact, she shied away from reading any gossip or glossy magazines given that nine times out of ten reports and information were incorrect.

But it was different when a man came right out and said what he was thinking…especially when he referred to her as stunning.

Growing up, she'd hated her hair and had often

coloured it more blonde than the red it had been back then. As she'd matured, the colour had settled to a deep auburn and she'd decided that it wasn't too bad any more. As far as looks went, she knew she wasn't displeasing to look at and while other men may have told her she was beautiful from time to time, it was still completely different from the way Dart had said it. It was as though the sight of her had taken away his breath and as far as she knew, she'd never really done that to a man before and definitely not one as enigmatic as her new colleague.

Dart lay back on his mat, not opening his eyes, not wanting to look at her any more in case he said other things that he shouldn't. Such as how he'd already thought about what it might be like to taste her luscious lips, to press his lips to the sweet silky smoothness of her skin.

Clenching his teeth, he crossed his arms over his bare chest. He needed to appear nonchalant, indifferent, to let her think that he doled out compliments like that every day to every woman he met. Yes, surely that would be the best way to handle the blunder he'd made and in the process, perhaps if he worked hard at it, he could regain more solid ground.

'You think I'm…' she tried again, and this time he cleared his throat.

'Stunning?'

'Yes,' she breathed.

'Of course—but, then, I suppose you already knew that.'

Emmy frowned, the tingles that had flooded her body at his words, at his initial reaction to seeing her with her hair loose, vanishing in an instant. There was a tone to his offhand confirmation, a tone that gave her a completely different impression from the one she'd garnered before, and this impression wasn't at all complimentary. 'What's that supposed to mean?'

'Oh, come off it, Emerson. You know you're gorgeous. You probably have ten men on a string at any given moment, all of them gushing and telling you how beautiful and wonderful you are.' Tarvon and Belhara had been paying her attention all day long, so why was it she seemed to care so much about the one little compliment he'd thrown her way?

Anger boiled within her and it took all her strength and training not to lash out and tell him the *real* truth. 'You know nothing about me, Dart Freeman.'

'I know you're in the press a lot.'

'*You* read the glossy mags?' There was a hint of derision in her tone as she turned and started to sift through her luggage for the things she required. 'Why do I find that so hard to believe?'

She was getting mad at him. That was good. Very good. He could deal with mad much better than her being all gorgeous and sexy and way too close. Mad was far better than her looking at him with those big blue eyes of hers, her hair floating around her head and shoulders, her petite, alluring figure drawing him in. Anger was far better than attraction and he continued to fan the flames of the fire.

'Think what you like. You don't know anything about me either.'

'I know you've come to the jungle, to the middle of nowhere, to lose yourself. You're hiding.'

There was a slight accusation in her tone, as though she dared him to deny it. Dart's eyes snapped open and he sat up to glare at her. She was kneeling on her sleeping mat, rummaging through her bag, torch temporarily at her side. The glow created an eerie atmosphere, the shadows all skewed and strange. It was exactly how he felt at the moment. He hadn't known Emerson-

Rose for all that long and already she was managing to distort his world.

'How could you possibly know that?' Someone must have told her. One of the villagers, but… He stopped. Only Jalak and…Meeree knew the real reasons he was here. Of course. He'd seen Emerson talking to Meeree on several occasions. Everyone knew that Meeree saw people in a different light and had the most amazing and accurate insights. Surely, though, she hadn't said anything about his past. She wouldn't do that. Meeree wasn't the vindictive, gossiping type.

'You're not so hard to read, Dart. I've been watching you, the way you interact with people, the PMA crew. The way you hold baby J'tagnan and look after his mother. The way you help where help is needed and how you contort those clever hands of yours into those shapes to make perfect shadow puppets.'

He could hear the wonderment in her tone and it washed over him with full effect. He wished she'd go back to being mad at him. On a 'keep your distance' level, it was easier for him to cope with.

'You give and you give and you keep on giving,' she continued. 'What you don't do is let anyone into the nice, neat little world you live in, the one that's shrouded by walls and darkness.' She'd found what she was looking for and flicked off the torch, plunging them into instant blackness.

It took but a moment for their eyes to adjust to the darkness. Dart didn't like the way she was making him feel—vulnerable. He lay back on the mat again, his arms still crossed protectively over his chest. 'I'd thank you kindly not to analyse me.'

'And I'd like the same courtesy from you.' Her words were slightly brisk, as though she was working hard at controlling that fire he'd been trying so hard to fan. 'I've worked too long and too hard to try and be my own person and even now, out here in a jungle hut in the middle of nowhere, I'm *still* getting hammered into a little box.' Her voice rose on the last part, the anger and frustration seeping through as she huffed around in the dark, changing her clothes and finally lying down.

Dart kept his eyes shut, trying not to listen to the sounds she made but failing miserably. He'd often slept in this hut over the years, with several other people, both men and women alike, and it had never bothered him before. Having Emmy close…the two of them together…alone… It most certainly bothered him.

He wasn't a great believer in instant attraction and had only experienced it once before in his entire forty-one years. That had been the first time he'd seen Marta. She'd been a nurse who had started working in the general surgical ward, on rotation from her hospital in Germany. She'd been feisty, fresh and absolutely fantastic at everything she did. She hadn't taken any of his dictatorial attitude, she'd broken through the walls he usually had in place to keep his distance from his work colleagues, and she'd captured his heart, all within a matter of weeks.

Now he was faced with another feisty, fresh female and the physical tug he felt towards Emmy was only increasing with every minute they spent together. It wasn't her fault she'd been born looking like a romantic princess, one that a knight in shining armour would gallantly save from whatever beset her.

Of course, she could well be using that beauty to get whatever it was she wanted from him, but even in the few short hours of their acquaintance Dart had to admit that she'd shown personality traits that seemed to contradict what he'd heard and seen of her in the media. Right now she was refusing to take any of his usual brisk attitude and she was showing courage by adapting to the situation and circumstances around her.

Apparently, he was hammering her into a box, or at least that was what she thought. Her words revealed much about her but his mind was too sluggish from a day that seemed to have stretched well past its usual twenty-four hours to process the concept thoroughly.

Admiration for her cooled his annoyance and when she was finally lying still, he tested the waters by saying, 'At least I hammered you into a *stunning* box.'

His words hung in the air for a brief moment before Emmy chuckled. 'True. Sorry about the outburst. I tend to find it difficult sometimes to bite my tongue.'

'We all do it,' he murmured, his body relaxing a little, his hands falling to his sides.

'My mother would be horrified with me.' Emmy sighed then smothered a yawn. 'Goodnight, Dartagnan. I hope you don't snore.'

'Likewise,' he said, wondering if it was going to be possible to get any sleep at all with her in the same hut, sleeping only a matter of a metre away. Thankfully, the night was supposed to be a warm one, which meant there would be no risk whatsoever of the two of them needing body heat to survive the night.

The instant he'd thought it, his eyes snapped open and his brain bolted back to life as visions of Emmy's body, snuggling closely to him, flashed into his mind, sparking his imagination. His arm beneath her head, her hair splayed out, tantalising his senses with its soft silkiness, her hand resting on his bare chest, her smooth fingers teasing the smattering of dark chest hair.

What was he doing? Why was he torturing himself like this? The answer came fast and hard on the heels of the questions.

He was drawn to her.

For some inexplicable reason, Dart didn't seem able to impose his natural ability to keep all working colleagues at arm's length. He had no idea why he was finding it so hard to treat Emerson-Rose as just another colleague but he was.

It was different with the villagers. To all intents and purposes, they were patients. Even if they didn't require his medical attention, they required other forms of healing, such as forgetting the troubles of their lives by watching shadow puppets. Laughter was a great tonic and one he'd used often to help his patients during his rotations in Tarparnii.

Emerson-Rose, however, wasn't a patient. Neither was she technically a colleague. Perhaps that was why he was having so much difficulty putting her into a box. A box. He recalled what she'd said about people always putting restraints on her abilities, on shoving her in a box without giving her the chance to prove herself.

From the way she spoke, it didn't sound as though she was all that happy with her life. Meeree had often told Dart that many workers from Australia came to Tarparnii because they were either running away from their pasts or trying to search out their inner self. By taking themselves out of their comfort zones, they would often come face to face with troubled insights and it was *how* they worked through these insights that would propel them forward.

From everything Emmy had said, it sounded as though she was searching for herself. Trying to prove herself. And it was then he realised it must be difficult to live in the shadow of famous parents.

He had an overwhelming urge to help her, to

let her know that out here she didn't need to be anything other than herself, who she was deep down inside. What would happen if he shared a bit of himself with her? If he showed her that not everyone was perfect, himself included?

'My parents weren't wealthy.' He said the words out loud, surprising himself as well as Emmy. 'We had to struggle for a lot of things in life. My medical training was funded by scholarships. They were hard times but we all pulled through, making the best of every situation.'

Emmy let his words hang in the air for a moment, his soft, deep voice relaxing her slightly.

'My parents are very wealthy,' she countered, her voice barely above a whisper. 'I had to struggle for their attention. My medical training is still a constant source of confusion to my parents. Financially, times have never been hard yet we hardly talk.'

She couldn't believe it when tears pricked behind her eyes. She'd never spoken to anyone so openly, so simply before. Her parents had sent her and her brother to therapists, had received reports on why she and Tristan had behaved the way they had, but still, it hadn't increased the time they'd spent with their offspring.

Emmy swallowed over the lump which had formed in her throat. 'Do your parents love you?'

Dart turned to look at her, even though he couldn't see her properly. 'Yes.' The word was easy to say because he knew it was true without a single doubt.

'Then you're far more wealthy than I'll ever be.'

Something had just happened between them. By opening the door to offer her some help, to try and show her that being true to herself was the best gift she could ever give herself, something deeper had seemed to connect them.

'Poor little rich girl.' He spoke with compassion. There was silence for a moment and he wondered whether he'd offended her. When she sniffed and sucked in a breath, Dart realised that she was crying quietly.

Without thinking, he quickly shifted, moving silently, closing the distance between them. In the next instant she was in his arms, her face buried in his chest, sobbing. With his free hand he reached into his pocket and pulled out a handkerchief, which she immediately accepted.

He didn't try to shush her, he didn't try to talk,

he didn't even stroke her back to calm her down. He simply held her and let her cry and that in itself, his pure kindness, only made her cry harder.

It felt as though thirty-two years of pain and frustration came pouring out of her. Emmy had no idea why she suddenly had no self-control. Perhaps it was the fact that she was here, in this jungle village, far from anything remotely familiar. She'd stepped outside of her comfort zone, stepped away from the tight control she usually held over her life, and with a few simple words, words that had revealed a lot about himself, Dart had somehow prised opened her floodgates.

The pain in her chest that came from crying, the way she sucked in a breath only to expel it with more sobs and tears somehow had a calming effect on Dart. He wasn't sure what to do but he'd seen his father at times holding his mother, just being there for her, letting her cry.

'Son,' he recalled his father saying softly to him one night when Dart had been extremely worried about seeing his mother cry. 'When times are harsh, when things are difficult and there often doesn't appear to be a way out, your mother needs to get it out of her system. She cries. I go and chop wood. We all have different ways of getting the frustrations out of our systems and then we can pick ourselves up, lift our chins high and start again.'

As Dart continued to hold Emmy, her sobs starting to slow a little, he realised she was just letting go. Like the rest of the media, he'd incorrectly assumed that simply because she was wealthy, she was happy.

'Money does not make the man,' his father had quoted more times than Dart could remember. His father had been quite a man and one Dart still continually strived to be like. He thought of his parents almost every day but in a more general way, doing his best to lift his chin high and start again. Although it had been six years since their deaths, six years since his world had come crashing down around him, Dart's ingrained perseverance had continued. It was a legacy from his father, as was the advice to simply stay still and let the woman cry.

Lying here in this hut, holding Emmy in his arms, he realised she wasn't just the socialite from the glossy magazines, or the student who had gone to medical school in search of herself, or the doctor who had come to this country to try and help others.

She was just…Emmy. A woman who had been hurt so badly by the people who should mean the most to her that she'd locked that core part of her away. Now that core was flooding, the tension was being released through her tears. Feeling rather melancholy himself, Dart adjusted the pillow beneath his head and closed his eyes.

He tightened his arms around her, protecting her, making sure she felt secure and safe. Of course, he had to work hard to ignore the way he liked holding her like this. The knight-in-shining-armour rule book stated clearly that sexual attraction played no part when offering comfort to a damsel in distress.

As her sobs changed to quiet hiccups, and her tears dried, he felt her breathing become more even, more controlled, and soon realised she was asleep.

He had no idea when he'd eventually drifted off, the sweet scent of Emmy's skin, the soft silkiness of her hair teasing his senses, lulling him into slumber, but when he woke, all he noticed was a throbbing pain in his right arm that was becoming unbearable.

Dart opened his eyes. The sun was starting to pour light into the hut, and he knew instantly where he was but had momentarily forgotten that he held the stunning Emmy Jofille in his arms. That was also the reason his arm appeared to be in pain, a lack of blood in that limb. As he looked at her, her head still resting on his shoulder, her long auburn locks splayed out along his arm, his gut tightened at the perfect picture she made.

When he'd first met her, he'd thought her beautiful. Hearing her talk about her reasons for being here, her desire to really help the villagers, had made him see her as intelligently beautiful. Now, after what she'd shared with him last night, he'd discovered she was as glorious on the inside as she was on the outside. She was stunning to look at and it now appeared she had a sweet and honest personality to match.

Where his life hadn't been easy due to poverty, hers hadn't been easy due to wealth. They seemed to be alike in so many ways yet completely different in others. Of one thing Dart was now sure. The woman in his arms wasn't Emerson-Rose Jofille, daughter of mogul Sebastian Jofille and joint heir to the Jofille family fortune. She was merely Emmy, a doctor who had come to

Tarparnii to help out, to throw light on the plight of these people and to raise awareness on the issues that plagued this pain-ridden country.

Pressure once more shot up his arm and he knew, with great reluctance, that he needed to move. He mentally went through the logistics of shifting without waking her before moving slightly and slowly.

No sooner had he turned than Emmy sat bolt upright, hair going everywhere as she scrambled to push it out of her face, out of her eyes.

'What? Huh? I'm up. I'm awake. What's the emergency?'

Dart's smile was instantaneous. 'There's no emergency,' he murmured, shaking and rubbing his arm to help increase the blood flow. 'I just had a dead arm. I didn't want to wake you.'

Emmy stopped, hands in mid-air, hair tangled everywhere. It was the least poised she'd ever been and yet seeing her like this only made his attraction to her increase.

She looked down at Dart, lying there, shirtless, rubbing his right arm as though to prove his words. Her eyes widened as she recalled the events of last night.

'Oh, no,' she groaned, and covered her face with

her hands, this time minus her hair, which she'd managed to at least push out of her eyes.

'What's wrong?'

'You. Last night.'

'Nothing happened, I swear.'

'I know nothing happened.' She dropped her hands with a hint of impatience. 'It's just…' She dragged in a breath and slowly let it out. 'I don't like to lose control.'

'Apparently.'

'What's that supposed to mean?' Annoyance coursed through her and she stood, straightening her cotton pyjamas as she went.

Dart chuckled. 'Nothing, really.'

'Then why is it so funny?'

'I'm not laughing *at* you, Emmy.'

'Well, you can't be laughing *with* me because I'm not laughing.'

His own frustration beginning to increase, Dart sat up, trying not to grimace as pins and needles flooded his arm. 'Look, I just meant that sometimes we need to lose control so that we can cope with what's coming next. Last night you let go and it was apparent that you hadn't let go for quite some time.'

'Are you calling me repressed?'

Dart rolled his eyes and stood, Emmy instantly backing towards the door. 'Stop putting words in my mouth.' And stop backing away from me as though I did something wrong last night, he added silently. 'If you're uncomfortable and embarrassed about what happened, about your loss of control or that I was here to witness it, then don't be.' He took two steps over to his own sleeping mat, snatched up his shirt and pulled it on, leaving the buttons undone. 'All I did was offer comfort and support and I won't let you make me feel like the bad guy. Be embarrassed all you want but don't go taking it out on me.'

With that, he pushed past her and walked out the door, allowing the screen to slam shut behind him.

Emmy stood there for a minute, biting her lip as contrition flooded through her.

CHAPTER SEVEN

THE morning was quiet as the village got on with their lives, Emmy delighting in each new experience, such as the way the villagers drew water up from the well and made a sort of porridge from dry ingredients, adding fruits and berries to the mix. Others were using a crude form of pestle and mortar, grinding down husks to make a powder, which they mixed with water into a dough. The dough was then kneaded and flattened out with their hands, before being cooked on a frying pan over a fire, the result being a crusty sort of flat bread.

Emmy and her crew, who were looking forward to catching up on their sleep, captured all of this on film, Emmy even helping out with some of the menial tasks. She laughed as the other women showed her what to do, the language barrier not seeming to be an issue. Dart watched her from the sidelines, J'tagnan in his arms as he gave the baby a bottle of milk.

'She is a very genuine person,' Meeree said, coming up beside him.

Dart didn't take his eyes off the bright, smiling woman who'd just accidentally rubbed flour on her forehead as she'd attempted to push a stray strand of hair out of her eyes. 'Yesterday I would have thought she was doing all this for the sake of the cameras.'

'And now?'

'She is genuine, just as you say.' J'tagnan finished his bottle and Dart shifted the baby around to his shoulder, patting the infant's back lightly.

'Your eyes have been opened.' Meeree sounded very impressed and Dart glanced at her.

'What do you mean?'

'That you see a different woman from the rest of the world.' Meeree's words were soft. 'She is lonely, Dartagnan. She has so much pain, so much hurt. You can help her with this.'

He tried not to baulk at the wise woman's words. 'I think she's more than capable of hiring someone to help her through, someone much better qualified than me.'

'It is not a matter of being qualified or not, child. It is not up to you that her heart has chosen you to confide in.' Meeree placed a hand on his arm. 'You are good at listening, Dartagnan. You will do what is right when she is ready.'

He looked back at Emmy, laughing with the other women, bonding with them, really reaching out to them. He recalled how frustrated she'd made him feel earlier on and frowned a little. 'She can be quite annoying at times.'

Meeree laughed and reached out her hands for the baby. 'That is the way it is meant to be. The trucks are arriving soon. Go and prepare, Dartagnan. I shall see to the baby and his mother.'

'Thanks.' Dart handed the baby over then leaned down and kissed Meeree on her cheek before heading off to do his job. He'd learned in the past not to question Meeree further when she made cryptic comments.

Coming to Tarparnii had helped heal a lot of personal wounds for him, losing his parents and Marta in a devastating bush fire being the main one. While he still missed them all very much, the way Meeree and Jalak treated all PMA helpers as one great big family had been incredible. Being with them, being a part of these people, had made him feel as though he wasn't so alone in the world, especially with all his nearest and dearest having perished.

By the time their colleagues returned from their impromptu callout yesterday, he had the supplies they would need all packed up inside the medical hut, ready to be loaded onto the trucks. Emmy walked into the medical hut as he was securing the last waterproof container.

'Oh, you're done.' She sounded disappointed.

'Wanted to film me packing things up? Getting ready to take medicines out to the sick and dying?' There was a clipped note in his tone, one even he was surprised to hear, but his walls were still up and firmly in place, especially after Meeree's words of wisdom. He was trying to keep his distance from Emmy, trying to ignore the invisible tug he felt towards her. Meeree's suggestion that he needed to help Emmy in a personal capacity only made him feel vulnerable and inadequate and they were not emotions he wanted to feel around her.

'No,' she replied simply, trying not to wince at his words. 'I wanted to help you.'

He shrugged. 'All done.' He reached for his hat, jamming it on his head, and went to heft the first container.

'Dart? Could you wait a second, please?' She spoke softly and clearly.

Dart straightened and turned to face her, leaning one arm on the top container, giving her his full attention.

'Uh… I just wanted to say that I was sorry about what happened this morning. You were right. I was embarrassed and it was a reflex action to take it out on you.'

'OK.'

He nodded once then turned to give his attention to moving the containers.

'I really am sorry,' she said again, not sure he understood that she was apologising for her uncalled-for behaviour. 'It's just I'm not used to being vulnerable, at least not in front of strangers.' She paused for a second, a small smile touching her lips. 'Although as we've basically slept together—literally—I guess I can't really call you a stranger any more and uh…'

He'd turned back to look at her again, his hands going into the pockets of his shorts, listening to what she was saying while trying to hide a touch of impatience. She'd apologised. He'd accepted. The trucks were waiting. There was work to do.

There was also the problem of how incredible

she looked, standing there, hands clasped uncomfortably in front of her, as though she was channelling all her embarrassment and nervous energy into her fingers. Her shoulders were straight, her head was held high. Perfect posture. Perfect breeding. She knew how to charm and to placate. She'd no doubt been taught at an early age how to put people at ease, how to smile at them and listen so intently, making them feel as though they were the only person on earth who mattered.

This time, though, the hands that she seemed to be twisting within each other were the only real indication of just how hard this was for her. In all honesty, though, Dart wasn't sure why she was prolonging her own torture. She'd apologised. He'd accepted. As far as he was concerned, that was all that was needed.

No explanations, no reminders of the way they'd woken up in each other's arms. No need to be standing here, alone, the air between them crackling with repressed tension and desire, desire he was doing his best to control, but when she looked all cute and alluring standing there, making sure he understood her apology…well, it only made him want to haul her right back into his arms and protect her from anything and everything this cruel world could throw at her. Clenching his jaw, he shoved his hands further into his pockets and tried again.

'It's OK, Emerson.'

'I just want to make sure you understand that I hadn't meant that to happen.'

'What? Waking up in my arms?' As he said the words, he watched as a tinge of pink started to colour her cheeks, only making her look more beautiful.

'Well…uh…there is that. I don't usually do things like that—crying, I mean. I'm normally quite in control of my faculties and so I can stifle any urge to sob my heart out.' She angled her head to the side and thought for a second. 'In fact, I can't ever remember crying like that before. Not even when I was a little girl.'

'Repression isn't good for the soul.'

'That sounds like something Meeree would say.'

'Or my mother.' The words were spoken softly, barely audibly, but even the mere mention of his mother brought a hint of reverence to his tone. It was Emmy's first clue that something was wrong. She'd been taught how to read people's body language, to know when they were uncomfortable, and she'd also been taught not to pry but to put them at ease. Prying and talking and discussing feelings were actively discouraged in her family.

Emmy could easily recall her own mother's words. 'Just our presence, just being there for people, is often enough to give them a hint of hope.' Lessons like that had made up an enormous part of her childhood. 'There are other people, professionals, who are trained to deal with people's problems, not us. In turn, no matter what anyone tells you, or what they attempt to share with you, your responses must always be polite yet impersonal.'

Emmy looked at Dart, seeing his own discomfort at being here, hearing the love in his voice as he mentioned his mother, and knew she wasn't going to give a polite yet impersonal response. She was trying to apologise to him, trying to get him to understand how embarrassed she was with her own behaviour.

'It's wonderful to see a grown man who's so close to his parents. The way you speak of them, it's clear you loved each other.'

Dart didn't say anything, he also didn't miss the past tense reference. Had she guessed? Given how good she was with people, she'd no doubt been able to figure it out. Still, he kept his gaze fixed on hers. Emmy tried not to be affected by it.

'Do you have any siblings?'

'No.' He knew he should turn, give his attention to the containers that needed to be loaded onto the trucks, but he couldn't look away from her, from those amazing blue eyes and the way she was making him feel. He didn't want to feel this way. He wanted to stay locked up in the pain from his past, from the great losses he'd suffered in losing those he'd loved most to the horrific flames of the bush fire.

She was drawing him out. He could feel that too and part of him wanted to run towards her, to see where this frightening natural chemistry that seemed to exist between them would lead. The other part of him felt guilty at even contemplating moving on, moving away from the memories of Marta, of the times they'd shared, of the life they'd planned together.

The memories of his parents were something that would always stay with him, for ever, no matter what he did in life, and somehow, right now, knowing Emmy didn't have a strong and loving relationship with her own parents, the need to share the parental love he'd been shown all his life seemed like the right thing to do.

'My parents couldn't have children, or so they thought. My mother became pregnant with me when she was forty-two. The birth was difficult. Both she and I almost died but by some miracle we survived.' His voice was soft, his words a little stiff, as though he wasn't one hundred per cent sure why he was telling her this, but he'd loved his parents so much and he hardly ever spoke of them, of the incredible people they'd been.

'It took her a good two years to recover from the ordeal but in the end she was a strong, upstanding woman.' A sad smile touched his eyes. 'She cared for her community, volunteered when she could, gratefully accepted handouts when they were needed. She would tell me that pride was a waste of time and all it ever did was get you into trouble. Loving people, caring for them, making a difference—those were the things that mattered most.'

'She sounds…incredible.' Tears had welled in Emmy's eyes as he'd spoken. Hearing his words, noticing he spoke in the past tense, only confirmed to her that something dramatic had happened to his parents. It only made her heart reach out to his even more.

'She was. So was my dad. We lived on the land, travelling from farm to farm, working as hired hands, cooking, shearing, mustering, whatever needed to be done.'

He was looking at her but not seeing her. Emmy didn't mind, honoured that he was opening up to her, that he was sharing this most special part of himself with her. It also made her own embarrassing outburst last night seem not so embarrassing. She'd opened herself to him and it was as though, to make her feel less uncomfortable, he was opening himself to her. He wasn't worrying about his pride, he was doing just as his mother had taught him.

'I didn't attend a proper school for years. I either joined in with the other country kids for School of the Air or took my lessons from my parents.' Dart smiled. 'I had a good life with them.'

'You make me feel quite envious.'

Emmy's words jolted him back into the present, back to where she stood, looking at him with glistening tears in her eyes. Had she moved closer? Had he? Somehow the distance between them seemed to have decreased and if he took another step forward, he'd be able to reach out and touch her, put his hands on her arms, draw her close, hold her gorgeous body against his once again.

He straightened his back, ordering his brain to shift back into protection mode, for the walls he usually kept firm around him to stand tall, to not let her in. The strange thing was that since meeting Emerson-Rose, he'd let her in far more then he'd let anyone in, especially during the past six years.

Marta's death had been something he'd thought he'd never recover from. When the tragedy had happened, everyone had told him that he'd feel better...in time. He hadn't cared too much for the counselling he'd received but now, so many years later, what he'd hardly dared to believe was actually happening. He could feel that instant tug, that instant attraction, that instant desire to press his lips to another woman's. Emmy. Emmy standing there and looking at him as though she felt exactly the same way.

Marta was in the past. Coming here to Tarparnii had helped him to get some distance so his heart could heal. Six years. Six long years he'd been without Marta, feeling as though he would never be truly alive again. And now here was Emmy.

He'd seen her in magazines, he'd flicked through newspapers and seen her picture on many occasions. He roughly knew the history of her family and never once had he been intrigued to look closer.

Now he couldn't help but look closer.

Before him stood a woman who had been given an upbringing most children would dream of. She'd no doubt had every toy, every piece of clothing, every gadget she'd ever wanted. Her parents had been able to pay for her education at the most expensive schools in the country. On graduating, they'd probably given her a car—and an expensive one at that. Anything and everything the world had on offer had been offered to her on a silver platter…and she was telling him that she was envious of his simple, often poverty-ridden lifestyle?

'Poor little rich girl.' He'd murmured the same words last night and still they were spoken with sympathy rather than derision.

He looked at the woman she'd become, the one searching for the truth of this world, the one looking to be accepted for who she was, the one who had the courage to be different, to change her fate.

Where he'd been commanding his senses to re-erect the walls he usually surrounded himself with, he found himself stepping towards her, almost desperate with the need to touch her, to reassure her that she was a woman of worth. She may not have received much in the way of true and honest love as she'd been growing up but she had the ability to give it, and that was an amazing achievement.

'Emmy.'

The one word spoken from his lips was enough to bring a mass of tingles to her entire body. She wanted to move towards him, wanted so desperately to reach out and touch him, to haul him close to her. Last night, as he'd held her in his arms, she'd never felt so secure, so protected in her life. She'd never felt worthy and yet somehow being here with Dart, having him look at her now as though he wanted to devour her but didn't want to push things too far, too fast, she liked him even more.

She'd wanted to apologise to him, to let him know that she wasn't the weeping type, to try and cover up her embarrassment at accepting his compassion. She'd tried to make him understand that she was usually a lot stronger than she was now, that she usually didn't fall apart at the slightest thing, but now, as he continued to move slowly towards her, her body starting to tremble in excited anticipation, Emmy couldn't believe that fresh tears seemed to be pricking behind her eyes again.

It wasn't because Dart was once more showing her compassion by accepting her apology—it was because he'd opened himself up to her, that he'd deemed her worthy of sharing his past, a very real and painful past. She'd been able to hear through his words just how much he'd loved his parents, just how much they'd loved him, and her need to feel a love that strong, that powerful, that consuming was rising within her.

When he stood before her, toe to toe, she looked up at him, her chin high so she could continue to gaze into those gorgeous brown eyes of his, eyes that she knew she could drown in, lose herself in and not care.

'Don't be envious.' His words were soft, his breath whispering across her skin. She closed her eyes, a slight tear squeezing out from the side of her eyelids, starting to slide down her cheek. Emmy swallowed, then gasped as Dart brushed the tear away with his thumb, the brief touch filled with caring.

She opened her eyes and looked up, wanting to say something, needing to let him know that she wasn't this crybaby that stood before him. 'I'm sorry for crying.' The words were choked, whispered through hoarse lips, but when he pressed a finger across them, silencing her, Emmy's heart pounded in triple time against her ribs.

'I've accepted your apology, Emmy. In my family, whenever someone gave a heartfelt apology, it was instantly accepted.' He shook his head. 'You don't need to apologise any more.' He brushed his fingertips lightly across her cheek, his gaze flicking between her eyes and her luscious mouth, which seemed to be beckoning him closer.

The need to taste her, to know exactly how it would feel to have her mouth against his, to experience the soft sweetness of her lips was consuming him. Nothing else mattered, not the past, not the present, not the fact that they were standing in a hut, in the middle of a jungle village in a country in the midst of civil unrest.

'Just like that?' she whispered.

Dart's heart was thudding painfully against

his chest, the blood pumping faster around his body, urging him forward, almost begging him to follow through on what came next.

'Just like that,' he confirmed.

'So simple.'

'Exactly.' He was still fighting, still trying to hold strong, still trying to remain in control of all his faculties, but it was becoming impossible to resist the lure of the woman before him. Last night he'd offered her compassion, he'd held her in his arms while she'd cried. This, now, was not in the least about offering her compassion. This was about a need, a powerful tug, an urge to have his mouth on hers, and it was a need he wasn't going to deny himself any longer. He wanted her. So simple.

Her pink tongue slipped out to wet her lips, the glossy moisture highlighting just how perfect those lips were, how necessary it was for him to taste them, to know how Emmy's mouth would fit with his own.

Forcing himself to keep a tight rein on his mounting desire for her, Dart lifted her chin a little higher while at the same time dipping his head, closing the remaining distance between them.

It was going to happen. This was the moment of inevitability. Her entire body seemed to be infused with tingles, with apprehension and acceptance. Her heart was pounding fiercely in her chest as anticipatory delight rose within her.

From the instant she'd seen him, she'd been drawn to him, and now, after what felt like a lifetime of loneliness, she was about to kiss a man who had come to mean so much to her in such a short time.

How was it possible to feel as though she knew his heart, could see his goodness, could want him to hold her close and never let her go when she'd just met him? She'd heard of love at first sight but she'd never in her wildest dreams ever thought she would experience it. Was she simply feeling this way because she'd stepped out of her comfort zone? Was it because she'd left her country, come here to this Pacific island nation to help out? Was it due to the genuineness of the people she'd met—Dart included?

Emmy pushed the questions away.

Now was not the time for questions. Now was not the time to try and figure out why this was happening or what it would mean afterwards. Now was about the way Dart was making her feel, making her burn with need as she never had before. He was a man who knew of her family, of her wealth, of her way of life, and none of it mattered to him.

That in itself was enormous for her to realise but as he continued to bring his mouth closer to hers, as his fingers at her chin continued to caress, burning a tingling heat trail with their simple, soft touch, Emmy's mind cleared of everything except the need pounding throughout her entire body.

'Emmy?' He whispered her name, their lips only millimetres apart, his breath mingling with hers, only intensifying the powerful yearning within them both. It took a few seconds for her sluggish mind to register that he was asking her permission, that he wasn't going to take from her something she wasn't freely giving. He was respecting her, giving her the choice, allowing her this last final moment to pull away, to deny him if that was what she wanted.

It wasn't.

Rising up on her toes, she removed his bush hat, desperate to close the remaining distance, and within that next half-breath she fused their mouths together in a searing kiss.

CHAPTER EIGHT

POWER. Passion. Perfection.

Within a split second of their lips touching, both of them seemed to sigh into the kiss. It felt as though they'd been denying themselves this release for an eternity when in reality it had been mere days since they'd met.

Gently, with restrained patience, wanting to mentally capture the moment, wanting to make it last for ever, to be permanently burned on his brain, Dart took his time, not rushing either of them. Their mutual touch was combined with a sense of time slowing down so that a few seconds seemed to last much, much longer. The tastes and flavours of her lips, combined with the tantalising pressure, was an aphrodisiac that powered the need for her throughout his entire body.

How was this possible? How could a woman who on the surface was so wrong for him feel so right deep within? Life had thrown him plenty of curve balls and this was another one he hadn't seen coming. His hand slid around her neck, her skin soft and warm to his touch, his fingers tantalised by the sensation of those silky locks, pulled back out of the way into a plait. What he wouldn't give to pull her hair free from its bonds and run his fingers through those glorious strands, much as he'd wanted to do last night but hadn't. Last night had been all about providing comfort, of being a friend to a person in need. This...what he was experiencing now...*this* was completely different. Last night, though, as he'd held Emmy in his arms, he should have realised that it had been a mere precursor to what he instinctively knew had been bound to happen.

There was an undeniable connection between them, a tug of awareness, knowledge of the heart, power in their eyes. Whatever it was that existed between them, had they done the right thing in giving in to the urge to touch, to taste, to try? The fact that they both felt it, the fact that it seemed to be seeded within each of them, was something incomprehensible given that they didn't know each other... Yet at the same time Emmy couldn't believe how connected she felt to this man who was playing havoc with her equilibrium.

His mouth seemed to know hers, his hands

seemed to understand the way she liked to be touched, his heart seemed to beat in unison with hers. It was a connection. An unbridled, unmistakable, uncanny connection that had somehow been buried deep within both of them, waiting patiently for the moment they would meet.

Where she'd expected his kiss to be filled with power, filled with the need to dominate, as had been her limited experience with the men she'd previously dated, he was gentle, caressing, probing as though, he too, wanted to try and understand what these sensations coursing between them meant.

How was it that he could simply accept what she had to give and not want more? How was it that he appeared to be letting her set the pace yet at the same time encouraging her not to pull away? Usually, because she was so wealthy, because she had so much in the way of material possessions, other men felt they had to dominate her, to show that they were better than her in an attempt to prove themselves worthy of her affection.

That wasn't the way it felt with Dart. Her wealth, her position in society, her heritage meant nothing to him. She was simply…Emmy. A woman he apparently wanted to slowly drive insane with his perfect mouth pressing perfect kisses to her lips, evoking wild and wonderful sensations of freedom and abandonment mixed with a sense of purpose.

It was the strangest sensation and one she wasn't in any hurry to have end. Where she'd half expected him to deepen the kiss, to increase the tension, to take her to greater heights, he didn't. Instead, it appeared he preferred to gently and thoroughly take his time, absorbing every new and exciting emotion that surrounded both of them.

It was delicate, sweet, wonderful torture and she wanted it to continue for ever. The world outside was forgotten, everything they were supposed to be doing was irrelevant when they could be doing this. There was no more embarrassment, no more need to talk about their pasts, no more denying that this indescribable chemistry existed between them.

At some point, his other hand had slid around her neck, tilting her mouth up so he could continue to give and take at the same time. Her breathing was erratic, her lungs begging for more oxygen, her body begging for more of his touch.

When he finally eased back, she was pleased

to note he, too, was sucking in air. At least she wasn't the only one affected by this tantalising scenario. Dart had been along for the ride, as much in the moment as she was, and that instinctive knowledge made her feel less agitated about what would happen next.

He rested his forehead against hers, his eyes closed as he allowed his body to settle back into a more normal rhythm...whatever that was. Since he'd first laid eyes on Emerson-Rose, his entire world had been knocked so off balance he wasn't sure he understood what a normal rhythm was any more.

Slowly, as his breathing returned to normal, so too came the realisation and knowledge about how these last few minutes might affect them. He'd kissed her. He'd kissed a woman—for the first time in six years, he'd given in to the urge to kiss another woman!

Guilt at moving on, guilt at not holding Marta's memory pure in his heart, guilt at having taken comfort from Emmy, started to swamp him and he dropped his hands back to his sides as though her touch now burnt him. At the same time he picked up his hat, straightened and took one giant step away, desperately needing distance between them.

What had he done?

He looked at Emmy, all dazed and languid, her blue eyes still showing the after-effects of the incredible kiss, her lips plump and red from the pressure of his mouth firmly on hers. Even now she looked dreamy, desirable and downright sexy, more sexy than any woman Dart had ever seen, and this knowledge only made him take another giant step away.

How could he have forgotten his past? How could he have become so caught up in the sensations and emotions he felt for this woman, a woman he barely knew, when Marta had perished, had died a horrible and painful death because he hadn't been there to help her?

He'd come to Tarparnii to help others, to continue Marta's legacy for always being there for those in need, and now here he was, helping himself to a woman who he wasn't sure he even liked. Did he like Emmy? He liked the vulnerability she'd allowed him to see. He'd liked the way she had the same drive as Marta, to really get in there and help those who needed it most.

Was that the reason he'd succumbed? Did

Emmy remind him of Marta? Was he projecting a lost love onto a woman who had the same sort of internal spirit? That need to give? If he was, then it was wrong. It was so wrong.

Swallowing, he shook his head and without another word turned and strode from the hut, leaving Emmy and the medical containers behind. She watched as the door closed behind him and it was only then that she seemed to snap out of the catatonic state that had held her, watching without being able to do anything as Dart had withdrawn from her.

Several emotions had flitted across his face. Confusion. Doubt. Anger. Still, there had been one emotion that had pierced her heart the instant she'd seen it in his eyes.

Regret.

Plain and simple. He regretted what had just happened between them even though it had been one of the most perfect moments of her life so far.

The way he'd looked at her, his touch, his mouth so incredible on her own. How could he deny what had passed between them? How could he just stare at her as though she was…nothing, and then walk away? She knew, without a doubt, with every instinct and fibre of her being, that he'd enjoyed that kiss, had wanted it, had needed it as much as she had. What she couldn't understand was why he was now trying to deny that. She'd seen the look in his eyes, had watched the emotions cross his face and heard the purpose in his stride as he'd turned and left.

Well…she wasn't as fickle.

She had been so into him, into that kiss, into the natural attraction that seemed to exist between them. However, if this was the way he was going to behave, she would harden her heart, the same way she'd had to against others in the past. Protection was paramount. Hadn't her parents shown her that at an early age? Protection for herself was what she must have at all times if she was going to move successfully through this world and not get hurt.

She dragged in a cleansing breath, centred her thoughts, squared her shoulders and hefted a medical crate in her hands, ready to head outside and focus on the job she'd come here to do. She was here to help others…and Dartagnan Freeman could go jump!

They took two transport trucks to the village filled with various medical supplies, tents and other bits and pieces they would need. The trucks had plenty of seating room in the back, the hard wooden seats not supporting any seat belts or comfort of any kind, the roof merely a canvas tarpaulin. Little baby J'tagnan and his mother came with them, the woman leaning her head against Dart's shoulder, the baby cradled safely in his arms.

He knew Emmy had spoken to both Meeree and J'tagnan's mother to gain permission to film mother and babe returning home. All had agreed it was an excellent idea and after she'd briefed Neal and Mike on what sort of shots she wanted, they'd left Jalak and Meeree's village.

As they drove along, the back flaps of the transport open to allow a breeze to surround them, the film crew sat on the end, cameras stuck out the back, filming anything and everything they could.

Emmy, on the other hand, was taking her own mental pictures of Dart, the man looking absolutely gorgeous as he sat there, protectively cradling the baby. A few times he glanced her way and she quickly looked somewhere else, trying to pretend he hadn't just caught her staring. She was still mad at him for making her feel so incredible. How could he do that? How could he make her feel as though someone in this crazy world really cared about her and then flip every emotion on its head and walk away from her with such ease?

She closed her eyes, trying to force her mind not to dwell on such things. Now was not the time. She was here in Tarparnii to do a job, to throw light on the situations and conditions these people lived in, not get romantically involved with a man who, although he kissed like a dream, really wanted nothing to do with her.

With her body moving in time with the truck as they rumbled along, Emmy zoned out to the conversations around her. She was becoming used to hearing the strange guttural sounds of the Tarparniian language and she was even starting to pick up a few more words.

She had attempted to learn a bit before her trip but that had been more in the vein of polite pleasantries. Right now, though, she had a few minutes to rest her eyes, to clear her mind from distractions such as Dart Freeman and go over the words she would use to describe this country. A lot of her work, a lot of the narrative for the piece would be added post-production once the film had been edited when they were back in Australia…and miles away from Dart.

The truck started to slow down and Emmy was surprised that they'd reached their destination so soon. She felt someone move past her and a tingle of awareness coursed through her body. When she opened her eyes, she wasn't surprised to find that Dart had handed the baby back to the mother and had made his way to the rear of the truck, his legs having briefly brushed hers as he'd passed.

The truck came to a complete stop and she prepared to get off the transport and into the village, anything to get her mind off the ever-present topic of Dart, but she found that this was not the village at all but a security checkpoint. Her eyes snapped open, her mind flicking into alert mode as several armed men in camouflage came to check out what was in the rear of the trucks, trucks that were painted with a big red cross on all three sides of the canvas surrounding their transport.

Fear started to tingle down her spine. Was this normal? Was this supposed to be happening? Flashes of a far-off event, of something that had happened in her past, long ago, came to mind as she watched the soldiers walk around the truck, their guns slung over their shoulders but their hands holding the butts of the weapons as though they were extensions of themselves, easily manoeuvred, easily used.

Her breathing started to increase and she found it difficult to swallow. Dart climbed from the truck and stood near them, handing over papers. Dart. Her heart pounded wildly against her chest as she watched him move, watched the way he held himself tall but relaxed. Dart. Anything could happen to him. They had guns, big, destructive guns, and Dart was right next to them.

Her mouth went dry and the drumming of her heart was loud, reverberating right through her so that she was having a difficult time focusing on what was being said. Time seemed to have slowed and a wave of sickness washed over her, distant memories, long forgotten, starting to return. If only Dart would get back in the truck. If only the men with guns would leave them alone. If only she could get her mind to focus, but her head was starting to spin.

When the soldier pointed to the camera and sound man, Emmy's anxiety increased. She parted her lips, her breathing becoming more erratic with each passing moment. Was something wrong? Was this supposed to be happening? Again, flashes of pictures from when she'd been five years old came instantly to the forefront of her mind.

She wasn't in a truck, she was in a town car. She wasn't with Dart, she was with Patrick. Emmy closed her eyes tight, trying to wash away the memory, but closing her eyes seemed to make it worse.

She had not long started school and was being driven by her chauffeur, Patrick. He'd slowed the car as he'd thought there were roadworks. There hadn't been. Patrick had wound down his window. She hadn't paid much attention, content to play with her doll in the back seat. Patrick had climbed from the car. He'd told her to stay put. Then a different man had climbed into the back of the car with her. He'd had a dark mask over his face and she'd only been able to see his eyes and his mouth. He'd had a metal thing in his hand. She'd seen Tristan playing with those things. Toy ones. Guns. This one, though, had looked bigger, scarier, deadlier.

A scream had worked its way up from her lungs and pierced the man's ears. He'd told her to stop making the noise and then had slowly slid the cold, hard edge of the gun against her cheek. Instantly, Emmy had done as he'd said. Another man had then climbed into the front seat of the car…a man who wasn't Patrick. Then she'd felt a sharp prick on the side of her neck and everything had gone blurry.

The kidnapping was something she'd repressed for a long time and while she'd known she might come across this sort of scenario, seeing men with guns, during her time here in Tarparnii, she hadn't expected to endure such a paralysing, terrifying reaction. She'd thought she'd dealt with the horrors of those terrible twenty-four hours she'd been stolen from her parents. Apparently not.

'Emmy?' Neal nudged her, bringing her firmly back to the present.

Her eyes snapped open and she covered her mouth with her hands to stop herself from screaming at his sudden touch.

'Emmy?' he said again, a little taken back by her reaction.

'What? *What?*' She was panting, perspiration peppering her brow as she tried to swallow over her dry throat.

'Uh…the papers,' Neal said hesitantly. 'Dart needs you to give him the papers that say it's OK for us to film in this country.'

It was then Emmy looked across and realised

that Dart was watching her with a curious but also clinical look. He'd moved. He wasn't surrounded by the men with the guns any more. He was leaning into the truck, his gaze trained on her.

'Are you all right, Emmy?' There was concern in his tone and she could only imagine what she looked like.

'Uh…' She made a quick and conscious effort to try and get her breathing under control as she bent to rummage for the papers in the backpack between her feet. It was the perfect opportunity to pull herself together, something she was glad she'd been taught to do quickly from an early age.

'A lady must be under control at all times, her emotions locked away in the privacy of her own mind. Giving to others, helping others is more important than helping yourself.' Her mother's words rang clearly in her mind yet again.

She handed the papers over to Dart, who in turn handed them to the soldier. Emmy's apprehension didn't disappear but she was at least pleased that she'd managed to calm herself down, to slow her breathing to a more normal pace, to be able to smile politely and do her job. That was until the soldiers ordered everyone off the transport.

'Why do we need to get off?' she asked, the fear quickly returning to her voice. Dart was helping people off and when she stood, he held out his hand to her.

'They just need to check everything over. There's nothing to worry about. It's all quite routine.' Although the instant she put her hand into his, he knew there wasn't anything routine about the repressed tension pulsating between them. Just the simple task of helping her down from the truck had his hormones going into overdrive. It was annoying because at the ripe old age of forty-one, he'd thought he had pretty good control over his hormones.

Not so when Emmy was near him.

As she stepped to the ground, she didn't let go of his hand, as he'd expected. When he looked at her, he could see the veiled panic behind her eyes. He'd thought he'd seen it a moment ago, before she'd bent to find her papers, but now he could see as clear as day that there was something going on here that was spooking her.

'Everything's going to be fine, Em,' he said softly. 'This is very routine. Happens so often that these guys...' he indicated the soldiers '... are getting to know me.'

She nodded at his words but the fear was still there. Dart put his free hand on her shoulder and looked intently into her eyes. 'Trust me, Emmy. I wouldn't let anything happen to you.' He might have no idea where the instant attraction had come from and he was far from being able to comprehend what it might mean, but what he did know was that the need to protect this woman was paramount. He'd felt it last night and he felt it now.

Dart continued to hold her hand as he spoke clearly to the guards, indicating that he was the man in charge. Emmy watched in complete fascination, the physical connection between them giving her more reassurance than anything else. Dart was here. He would protect her. She would be fine. No one was going to take her this time. No one was going to hurt them. The soldiers, for all their gun-carrying, seemed to be quite reasonable, not like the terrifying kidnappers who had given her nightmares for such a very long time.

There didn't appear to be any animosity between the guards and Dart, both parties smiling now and then, as though they'd gone through this drill many times before. What Emmy couldn't believe was the way her heart seemed to swell with pride and admiration for Dart. He was a commanding presence. Whether he was discussing and negotiating with a man holding a gun, performing shadow puppets with his hands or pressing his lips passionately to her own, he was the type of man to do everything to the best of his ability.

It wasn't long before they were all back on their cargo transport, heading off towards their destination, the armed guards waving and smiling as they drove away. It had seemed surreal and she knew her crew had captured it all on film. It also brought home the fact that while there was fighting going on all around them, there was also some sort of order in the way things were organised. There were innocent people living in this country, people who required medical attention, and it appeared PMA was allowed to provide that attention.

Dart had reluctantly let go of her hand as he'd helped her back into the truck, also giving his attention to J'tagnan and his mother and other members of the PMA crew. Everyone had shuffled seats from where they'd previously been sitting and this time Emmy realised that the only available seat left for Dart was the one next to her. After bidding a polite farewell to the soldiers, he turned and made his way towards her, carefully easing his tall frame onto the wooden bench. Neither of them spoke for a few minutes, Emmy trying hard not to be affected by the way his shoulder kept brushing against hers as the transport rocked gently to and fro.

'Are you all right?' His voice was quiet and smooth yet she could hear him quite well over the noise of the truck engines.

'Fine.'

'Something happened back there. Are you sure you're OK? You really did look terrified.'

Emmy swallowed. 'It's OK. I'll tell you some other time. Nothing to worry about now.'

'Sure?'

She glanced around them. 'These are hardly the surroundings.'

He held her gaze but knew she was right. 'OK. So long as you're all right.'

'I am.'

'Good.'

An awkward pause settled over both of them and Emmy called on her finishing-school training once again in order to remain calm. 'Agitation is not a becoming quality for a lady.' Her mother's words rang in her head and Emmy folded her hands into her lap, straightened her back and took a soothing breath...then wished she hadn't.

The scent of whatever it was Dart wore teased at her senses, the spice, the earthy goodness and the plain heat coming from the man mixing itself into a powerful aphrodisiac. Her body tingled with awareness, goose-bumps rippled down her arms and legs, and when his warm thigh brushed against her own, she received a jolt of delight.

Memories of his mouth on hers, of his arms holding her, of the way those kisses had been the sweetest, most seductive kisses of her entire life, flooded through her and she did her best not to gasp at the contact. So much for remaining calm!

'I should have told you about the checkpoint so you weren't worried.' Dart spoke softly, breaking the silence.

Emmy swallowed. 'It's fine.' She waved his words away. 'All part of the experience of being somewhere different.'

'Huh.' He nodded, easily seeing through her pretence of appearing calm and in control. She was a person who needed to be in control, to prove herself, to show the world that she was much more than just another rich heiress. And she was, he realised. The more he came to know her, the more he liked what he found.

As he glanced down at her, his gaze settled on her mouth and the memory came back to him of just how sweet, how wonderful and perfect she'd tasted…the feel of her close to him…her scent winding itself about him, just as it was now. Did the woman have any idea just how she was making him feel, sitting this close, their bodies jostling together as the truck continued to rumble its way to their destination?

Desire buzzed through him. He clenched his teeth, doing his best not to touch Emmy more than he was at present, even though he was almost desperate to put his arm around her shoulders and hold her close to him, have her turn her face up towards his so that he could lower his mouth to hers and ki—

'It reminds me of my time in Outback Australia.' Emmy's words cut across his thoughts, bringing his mind back to the present.

'What does?'

'Being out here.' She spread her arm, indicating the beautiful scenery they were driving past. 'It's so vast, so different from our normal lives. Tight communities, supporting each other, helping out where needed.'

Dart cleared his throat, his mind now back on track. 'Were you in the Outback for another television assignment?'

'Yes.'

'Whereabouts did you go?'

'Sorry?'

'In the Outback. Have you been to several places or just one…community?'

'I did a three-part series on outback doctors. I spent quite a bit of time in Didjabrindagrogalon in Western Australia and also up at Dingo Creek and Blaytent Springs in the Northern Territory.' She smiled as she spoke. 'Everyone rallies around, doing what needs to be done, just as you and your team do in the villages. They make house calls, which, to all intents and purposes, is what I guess we're doing today—driving to another village to help out.'

'Exactly.' He pointed to the scenery as they drove along the ungraded road. 'Although there aren't so many trees in the outback.'

'No.' She smiled as she looked at the lush, green jungle, the rain having come once more, falling softly but constantly. The humidity started to rise and with it came the annoying insects. 'And in the outback, the heat tends to be dry, with flies being the dominant insect.' She turned and looked up at him…and he wished she hadn't.

Her smile was delightful, the curve of her lips only enticing him more than he cared to admit. Her eyes sparkled with an intensity he didn't want to know about. Her flowery scent wound its way about him, making him crazy for her.

How was it that in the past he'd been able to easily fight attractions to other women, never once making a dent in his resolve to never marry and to keep Marta's memory alive? What was it about Emmy that made him want to slip his arm around her, pull her towards him and press his mouth to hers once again? Why should she be any different from other women?

Because she was.

There was no logic in the answer, just as there was no logic in the question. He was attracted to her and perhaps the sooner he stopped trying to deny it, the sooner he would be able to gain control over this temporary infatuation and get back to his normal life where he could happily brood about his lost love all he wanted.

'Please don't look at me like that, Dart,' Emmy said softly, and it was only then he realised he was still staring at her.

'I can't help it.' The words were out of his mouth before he could stop them. He made no effort to touch her, to hold her hand, to cup her face in his and press his mouth to hers, which she was becoming desperate for him to do.

'I'm drawn to you, Emmy. Believe me, I don't want to be but I am.'

She frowned a little at that, feeling a touch insulted. It carried through in her tone. 'Good to know reluctance is still alive and well.'

'Look, all I meant was that we come from different worlds. You'll be gone in another few days, back to Australia, back to your life in front of the camera, working for a television network and doing…whatever else it is that you do.'

His tone, his words made it all sound so glamorous when in reality, it was a way she'd devised to live so no one knew just how lonely she really was.

'Nothing.'

'Pardon?'

'I do nothing.'

Dart frowned. 'Yes, you do. You do excellent work for charities and…and you help people just by being there, by listening to them.' He felt a little out of depth as he spoke, given that all he really knew of her life was the few snippets he'd caught in the press over the years. Still, he didn't want her to think that he'd been trying to attack her with his words. Quite the opposite.

'Your story here, what you're filming now, will help people in Australia to know all about Tarparnii and how they can help out. Australians are a giving people and always come through for a good and noble cause such as this. You're a big part of that, not only giving of yourself but making sure issues aren't swept beneath the carpet.'

'Now you're making me sound like a saint and that I am definitely not.' There was a hint of hope in her tone, the desolation starting to slip away, and she couldn't believe how much of an influence Dart's words had on her. His opinion of her mattered. That's what she realised in that moment. She cared, probably far too much, what he thought of her.

Pleased he'd made her smile again, Dart took her hand in his. 'Emmy, I think you're an incredible woman and, yes, there is an attraction between us—a rather strong one given the past twenty-four hours—but—'

'We can't let it get the better of us,' she finished for him, nodding slowly, trying desperately not to react to the warmth of his hand. Just one simple touch from him and she was again reduced to a quivering mass of uselessness.

'I can't do my job properly and neither can you,' he continued, rubbing his thumb tenderly over her knuckles.

'We need to concentrate,' she agreed, and looked from their entwined hands up to his face, his brown eyes reflecting the deep and powerful sensations he felt for her. It was almost enough to make her renege on the words she'd just uttered. What she wanted was for him to lean down and press his mouth to hers, to kiss her not with the soft sweetness from this morning but with the powerful, animalistic need that she could feel was simmering beneath the surface in both of them.

She swallowed. 'Friends?'

'Friends is good.' He gave her hand a little squeeze and smiled, hoping she couldn't read in his expression that he wanted to be far more than just friends with her.

As the trucks slowed, turning off the road, such as it was, and heading into the jungle towards the village, Dart reluctantly let go of Emmy's hand before both of them looked straight ahead, willing themselves to focus on the job at hand but both finding it impossible to think of anything else but each other.

CHAPTER NINE

FOR Emmy, arriving in a different village, one that was much smaller than Jalak and Meeree's, was an adventure. She greeted the people in the way Meeree had taught her, holding both their hands and moving them in a little circle, as was the traditional Tarparniian greeting. She was able to greet their hosts in their native language and even managed to pick up a few words here and there as other people gathered around, eager to be on camera.

As Dart watched her, he realised that Emmy was indeed a great diplomat. She was happy, joyful and utterly charming, the village elders warming instantly to her. She could put people at ease with her sweet smile, the language barrier not necessarily a barrier.

She was a giver. Emerson-Rose may have been raised by her parents to be the perfect hostess, the perfect patroness, the perfect representative for her father's company, but she was now using those skills to bring brightness and sunshine to a small village in the middle of a country where there wasn't usually a lot of happiness. She was quite a woman.

'They're not shy,' he heard her say, laughing, as the children all danced and jumped up and down, wanting desperately to be filmed. After a few more minutes she left her camera and sound colleagues to do their thing and went to help Dart and the others set up the large canvas tents that would be their clinic rooms for the next two days.

'Is Tarvon in charge of this mission, too?' she asked quietly as she hefted a medical container from the truck, walking alongside Dart who was carrying two containers at once. She tried not to focus on the way the manual labour tautened his incredible upper body, his muscles pressing against the material of his cotton shirt as though straining to break free.

'Yes. This will be his final test, so to speak. A two-day clinic.'

'You're the examiner?'

Dart shrugged nonchalantly. 'You could put it that way. Tarvon is incredibly talented and has been working both here and overseas with PMA for a few years now, but he's never wanted to take a leadership role until recently.'

Emmy nodded. 'How interesting. I had no idea how extensive the training was for a supervisory role.'

'Journalistic instincts at work?'

'It's good to know that PMA takes its medical responsibilities seriously. That's something that should be reported in the segments we'll be putting on air.'

'Agreed.'

They put the containers down and continued setting things up—tables, wash basins, towels, medical supplies. Just after midday the set-up was completed and the team ready for business. They all sat down and had a quick lunch, eating the dry supplies they'd brought with them, as well as having a quick cup of instant coffee.

'Do you usually bring all your own food?' she asked.

Dart nodded. 'It's wrong to come into a village, offer help and then expect to be fed. PMA provides us with what we need, even if it is freeze-dried. The villagers, especially in a smaller village like this, sometimes don't even have enough to feed themselves.'

Emmy nodded and finished off her coffee.

'So? Are you ready?' Dart asked her as they started to pack away the food supplies.

'For?'

'The clinic.'

'Will I be working with you again?'

'No. You're a qualified doctor, Emmy. You've shown me that you're more than capable of helping out.'

Emmy stilled at his words, a little surprised that he was giving her this opportunity.

'If you have a problem with the language barrier, just ask one of us, or, if we're busy, P'Ko-lat can translate for you.' Dart continued, unaware that he'd said anything to stun Emmy.

Confusion and uncertainty, mixed with determination and honour, flooded through her. 'You really think I can do this?' The question was soft and only then did Dart look at her.

'Of course I do. If I didn't think you were skilled enough, I'd say so.'

Emmy couldn't believe the amount of pride she felt at his words. Dart believed in her. Dart thought she was more than capable, skilled enough to handle patients of her own. She knew how tough conditions could be out here and he thought she was ready.

'Thank you, Dart. I won't let you down.' Her words were filled with happiness as well as urgent determination, her hands clasped excitedly before her.

'Good, because it's going to be one humdinger of a clinic. Just when there's a lull, another group of people come.'

'How do they know it's on? I mean, there's no way to advertise. Do they use calendars? Day planners?' She laughed at her own words.

'Word of mouth has always been the most effective form of advertising and as far as calendars go, it's more a case of every fourteen sunrises, there's a clinic, so to speak.'

They would all be working in the large tents together, several areas having been set up for the patients to be treated. It was similar to footage she'd seen on television of medical tents during the Second World War.

J'tagnan and his mother were sitting in a hut with some of the other women, the baby having been strapped into a papoose to his mother's front, making it easier for her to carry and care for him. Dart had already told Emmy that they would be travelling to J'tagnan's village tomorrow where the new babe would have a welcoming ceremony.

'Something else for your cameras to film. It will surely tug at a lot of heartstrings when people in Australia see just how precious each child is here. Each village takes care of its own and there is no one family more important than any other. Everyone has a job in the village, everyone takes care of each other. It's the truest form of a community.'

Emmy was still reflecting on his words, seeing for herself the way people were welcomed, the way everyone was supported. It was an amazingly simple way of living. No rich, no poor... just equals.

As people started to arrive and the clinics officially began, Emmy also noted that all the people in the host village allowed others to go before them. Again, it was simply another indication of how polite the Tarparniians were and how they cared for each other.

There were several cuts, scratches and bruises to be attended to, which, in a general medical practice in Australia, would be treated in the common way, but out here, where there was a

lack of running water, clean bandages and constant hygienic practices, it meant that a simple
cut or scratch could turn sceptic quite easily.

Emmy lost count of the number of wounds she
debrided, bandaged and issued doses of penicillin
for to guard against infection. Her earlier enthusiasm was replaced with exhaustion as well as a
quiet sense of achievement. P'Ko-lat had been
great in leading patients to her and explaining
exactly what their medical needs were.

So many came for immunisations, a lot of pregnant women came for checks on their babies,
wanting reassurance from the doctors. A large
proportion of their patients were female, older
men—usually coming along to protect the women
but really wanting to receive treatment for one
thing or another—and children of all ages.

'Why aren't there young men?' Emmy asked
Dart during one of their breaks. They both ea-
gerly sipped cups of fresh nectar that the villagers
had prepared for them as a gesture of thanks.

'Young men are the same the world over. They
think they're invincible.' He smiled, then sobered.
'They've gone to earn money. Either taking jobs
in the larger cities or joining the soldiers to help
fight for their country.'

'That makes no sense at all.'

Dart shrugged. 'If you start to ask why, if you look for rationalities in any war, your head is likely to explode.' He finished his drink. 'And then, Dr Jofille, it will be up to me to patch you back together again.'

'I can think of worse things,' she said softly, and wasn't sure he'd heard as he didn't immediately look her way. Slowly, though, he raised his head and their gazes met. Brown eyes met blue as the world around them fell away. How was it that she was able to make him forget everything but the burning need and desire coursing through him?

They'd already agreed that this instant attraction was going to lead them nowhere and that they were far better off being just friends, getting to know each other more, yet he had a sudden flash of insight that they might not be able to turn their growing feelings for each other off so conveniently.

'This is quite intense, isn't it?' Emmy was the first to speak as she put her cup down and walked towards him. Dart found that he couldn't move. His eyes were trained on hers, his body aware of the graceful moves she made, his head filled with only her.

'Friends. We said we'd be friends.' His words were quiet and he idly wondered why right at this moment there weren't any other people around in the food hut. Why couldn't they be interrupted? Why couldn't they focus on what they were supposed to be doing?

'Friends is good.' She reiterated his earlier words but didn't stop advancing towards him. 'I'm no expert, Dart, but I have the feeling that attraction like this doesn't come along every day.'

'No.'

'Sometimes it's one-sided.'

'Sometimes it's not.' His gaze was still riveted on hers, conscious of the way his body's response was increasing with every move she made towards him. Heat ran up and down his spine and his body tensed, his jaw clenching as he worked hard to control the effect she had on him. The only thing that made him feel slightly better was the fact that Emmy apparently felt the same way.

He didn't think she was the type of woman to lead a man on, especially not in their present surroundings. Most people joined PMA with not only a need to provide medical assistance where it was required most but also as a means of escaping their own lives. On a personal level, Dart knew exactly how that felt, given that in helping others, it helped him to forget the pain of his own past.

They most certainly didn't join with the intention of finding a life partner. Besides, he had to keep reminding himself that Emmy wasn't here as a member of PMA but was attached in a journalistic capacity in order to film the life of the Tarparniians, and while her motives for the documentary might be pure in that she really did have the desire to help, he would still be wise to keep his distance. Both of them were leaving the country very soon. His current contract with PMA was up and Emmy's week-long project would end. Being here, away from the rigours and confusion that accompanied everyday life in Australia, wasn't really *real*.

Yet as she continued advancing towards him, her sweet, inviting scent reminding him of lazy relaxed evenings, he realised he was having trouble keeping rational thoughts uppermost in his mind. Her eyes told him that she wanted his mouth against hers, her lips parted as though in complete agreement, her body swayed slightly as she sashayed towards him.

'This is ludicrous,' he managed to choke out,

shoving his hands into his pockets to stop himself from touching her.

'I know, and at the same time I can't seem to help myself.' Her breathing had increased and the closer she inched towards him, the faster her heart seemed to pound. He wasn't walking away. Surely that was a good sign. He wasn't turning on his heel and stalking from the hut, even though she knew he had every right to do that.

In some ways she wished he would, to have the self-control she most certainly didn't seem to have, but on another level she was ecstatic that he wasn't walking away, that although he stood there with his hands in his pockets, no doubt to help him to resist touching her, he still wasn't about to turn tail and run.

She had to admit she found it powerfully exciting being the one to pursue a man. Usually, she had men fawning all over her but she knew that was because they were more interested in her money than her on a personal level. Not so with Dart. She knew money meant nothing to him, that strong character, good morals and ethics were far more important to this man who had such sadness behind his eyes.

'You look at me as though you can't get enough

of me. I can feel your gaze on me, like the sun kissing my skin. It's there as I talk to other people, as I move around the village, as I treat patients.'

'Er...sorry.' He cleared his throat, his words soft. 'I don't mean to make you uncomfortable.'

Emmy smiled at that. 'You don't.' She came to stand before him and reached up to brush a lock of hair back from his forehead. 'You make me feel special, desirable, sexy.'

'Emmy, don't say things like that.' His tone was husky, he couldn't hide it.

'Why not? It's true, Dart.' She lifted one of his hands from his pocket, pleased when he didn't stop her, and placed it at her waist. This was the most forward she'd ever been with any man and while part of her couldn't believe what she was doing, the rest of her felt completely liberated, as though here was a man she could be completely honest with and he wasn't going to push her away. All her life, with her parents, with her nannies and even, to an extent, with her brother, Emmy had been required to keep the real her, the part that was filled with such yearning, such need, hidden from people in a bid for self-preservation.

Now, here, with Dart, she felt as though she could finally be free of that, be herself, be the real Emmy who had been sitting in the dark for far too long.

'I have been restricted by what I can and cannot say for most of my life.' She continued to speak softly, gently touching, caressing his face, learning the contours and committing them to memory.

'If I said one thing wrong at a press conference, it would make headlines the next day. If I got drunk or acted up, it would make the second top news item. I'm not a rebellious sort of person, Dart, never have been, but I've been bound by such tight bonds for far too long and here, now, being with you…' she trailed her fingertips across his forehead and down his cheek, the tingling stubble of his whiskers only heightening the sensations coursing through her '…seeing the way you look at me, feeling the caress of your gaze, knowing that you're interested in me—in *me*—not my money, experiencing the powerful and drugging sensations when you kiss me…' She sighed, her eyelids fluttering closed for a brief second, showing exactly how she felt when his mouth was on hers.

Her breathing had increased even more now and as Dart continued to watch her, his gaze flicking between her mouth and her eyes, the emotions became even more intense. She slipped her tongue out to wet her lips, the action bringing forth a groan of deep-seated need from Dart. It only gave her more confidence.

'Friendship is important, Emmy,' he managed to choke out, his words brushing against her lips they were so close.

'We can be friends,' she insisted. 'I was never a believer in instant attraction but when it hits you like a slap to the face, it's hard not to notice. It's as though I've known you a lot longer than I have. I can't explain that and I've stopped trying to understand it. I can't help the way you make me feel, and from the moment we met, I've been fighting it,' she explained in a rush, her words tumbling over each other as she tried to make him comprehend just how he made her feel.

'I don't want to fight it any more, Dart. I like feeling the way you make me feel. I like being around you.' She edged even closer, his hand at her waist now sliding further around to rest in the centre of her back. His other hand was still in his pocket, clenched tightly as though he needed to maintain some control over what was happening here.

'I like the tingles which course through me

when you touch me. I like the heat that starts as a slow burn then works its way up to a frenzy when your lips are against mine.'

'Shh.' Dart closed his eyes, wondering how on earth he was supposed to fight against this. 'Stop saying things like that.'

'Why?'

'Because it makes it more complicated.'

'Why do we need to be rational?' Her words were enticing him further, drawing him closer. Never before had he been so seduced by a woman as he was now. He'd watched her in the village today, watched the way she gave one hundred per cent of her attention to whomever she was with, whether it was a patient or a member of the village community. She cared. She really cared about them and now, as she gave him that same undivided attention, he knew deep within his heart that she really cared about him and what she was saying wasn't just words.

And that was the major part of his problem.

She wanted to get to know him better. She wanted to be real friends, not just colleagues. She wanted to probe into his past, to get him to open up to her. He had no idea why but he simply knew, instinctively, that agreeing to be friends with Emmy definitely meant more than colleagues who shared a few tales from their pasts as they sat around the hut of an evening trying to unwind from a full day's work.

He could freely admit that he wanted to kiss her now more than anything. He wanted to be near her, to hold her against his body, to feel the way she responded to him, to know that whatever he did say to her, whatever he told her from his past, would stay between the two of them. Friends. She wanted to be friends but it appeared she wanted to be friends who had a certain level of intimacy.

'You intrigue me, Emmy.'

She smiled at his words. Her mouth was so close to his, he *felt* the sides of her mouth tug upwards as he spoke. 'I'm going to take that as a compliment.'

'You should. You're a remarkable woman and the fact that I'm intrigued means I want to know more. That doesn't usually happen to me and most definitely not with colleagues, but there's more to think about than just this moment here and now. We can become friends. We can talk, we can share, we can…kiss.' He shook his head, the movement so small it was almost imperceptible.

'We will leave this country in a matter of days,

both to return to our lives in Australia. Our very *different* lives. I've seen it all before. People work together here, they go through some stressful and often life-changing experiences, and when they return home, they're different and the people around them, the people who are in their daily lives, don't understand what happened. The couples are usually from different States, sometimes different countries, so they find it even more difficult to see each other, and even if they do live close to each other, normal life has a way of changing things. Here, everything is amplified. Back home, you may not feel the same way about me.'

And there it was, she thought. In a nutshell, Dart was letting her know that he thought that when they returned home, *she* would change. *She* would get swept up in her 'different' world and not want to be with him. There was nothing she could say at the moment that would make him think any different and so she decided to *show* him just how important he was becoming in her life.

'You know what your problem is?' she asked.

'What?' The one word was defensive.

Emmy laced her fingers at the back of his neck and urged his head down. 'You talk too much.'

With that, his mouth was once more pressed to hers in another heart-stopping, mind-spinning, earth-shattering, axis-altering kiss... And he realised there wasn't a thing he wanted to do to stop it.

CHAPTER TEN

THE woman was incredibly alluring, drawing him into her life by the sweet way she touched him. She tasted of promise and hope and it was those very things he'd been searching for to fill the lonely void in his life for a long time. His past was his past. He knew that. He'd accepted that but in some ways he hadn't expected to ever move on.

Then he'd met Emmy.

Dart slipped his arms about her, drawing her closer, needing her closer. Everything she'd said had been correct. The need that burned between them was only going to intensify and was it wise to ignore it? Friendships could survive on a more intimate level, couldn't they? As the kiss intensified, his mind cleared of all thoughts except how she tasted, so sweet and full of flavour, so intoxicating.

'Emmy.' He murmured her name as his mouth broke free, dragging in breath but still unwilling to completely break the embrace, pressing small butterfly kisses along her jaw to her ear, nibbling at her earlobe, drawing in the scent she wore and nuzzling her neck, making him wonder if he was ever going to be able to let her go when they returned to Australia.

She wrapped her arms about his neck, giggling slightly at the way he continued to kiss her neck. 'You're tickling me.'

'I like your laugh. It's so free,' he whispered into her ear.

Emmy sighed into the embrace, closing her eyes and wondering if she'd ever felt this happy before. Dart was holding her close, whispering sweet things in her ear, pressing light, tantalising kisses to her skin, and she wanted more. 'I like you making me laugh,' she returned.

Dart chuckled at this. 'Are we forming a mutual admiration society?' There was the sound of distant thunder, which they both knew wasn't really thunder but more people coming to the small village, people in need of medical treatment. He'd snatched a few moments with Emmy and they were moments he knew he would cherish, being able to hold her this close, to breathe in her scent, to kiss her just as he'd dreamed of doing.

'I think we're already charter members.' Emmy

laughed and tightened her hold on him, her laughter ending on a sigh. 'They're coming, aren't they? More patients. More treatments.'

Dart eased back slightly and looked down into her gorgeous face. 'It's not too much for you, is it?'

'Good heavens, no. I didn't mean to imply that I was exhausted or tired of treating patients. Not at all.'

'That's good because you're such a natural with them all. Not even the language barrier seems to be stopping you.'

'Thank you.' She pressed a kiss to his cheek. 'I only meant that the arrival of a new round of patients means less time for us to become better friends.'

Dart shifted, bringing his hands to rest on her shoulders. Emmy slowly but very reluctantly slid her hands down to rest on his chest, her fingers memorising every contour. 'Friends,' he agreed, although they both knew that even with this last kiss the landscape between them had changed once again.

He'd just dropped his hands back to his sides when Gloria poked her head into the food hut. 'There you two are. Ready for round two?'

'Lead on,' Emmy said, feeling more confident, not only in her work but in her burgeoning relationship with Dart.

That night they slept in tents. All the medical staff, along with Emmy and her crew, were squashed into two of them. Dart noticed that Emmy made sure her sleeping area was right next to his and later in the evening, when the others were sound asleep, she snuggled into him.

It was a small slice of heaven, a slice he'd thought he would never know again. Emmy had awakened feelings he'd thought long gone. Gone when Marta had perished, her life snuffed out by the same fire that had claimed the lives of his parents. His world had gone from happily structured to destructive disarray.

It couldn't last. It *wouldn't* last. He was at least honest enough with himself to realise that. They came from two completely different worlds, not only geographically because they lived in different States back in Australia but also because they came from opposite sides of the tracks. If he allowed himself to follow this path, to think that there could be anything remotely permanent between Emmy and himself, he would end up hurting both of them.

There could be no future for them. She was a public figure, a high-profile person not only in the world of television but in the fast and furious world of the rich and famous. He was a doctor who preferred to spend his time working in the middle of nowhere where life ran to a more simple rhythm. Here he could help others, focusing on giving rather than on looking inward to his own life.

Emmy may have shown him that he wasn't as dead inside as he'd originally thought but the fact of the matter remained that there could be no future for them.

He closed his eyes against the truth, tightening his hold on the woman who had come to mean so much to him in such a short time. Soon they would return to Australia, to their own worlds, where they would slot nicely back into their own lives, their time together, this very night, becoming a pleasant but distant memory of a perfect moment.

The instant the words came to mind, Emmy started to flinch a little, her breathing increasing and as Dart looked down at her, he saw her brow furrowed into a frown. 'No,' she whimpered. 'Leave me alone.' When she started to tremble, Dart tightened his hold on her, his heart pierced by the thought that she was dreaming such terrible things. Was someone trying to get her? Hurt her?

'Shh. It's OK, Emmy. I'm here. I've got you,' he murmured soothingly, and dropped a kiss on her forehead, the possessiveness he'd felt towards her over the past few days increasing yet again. 'I won't let anything happen to you.'

At his words, Emmy's brow relaxed, her breathing returning to a more normal rhythm as she snuggled in closer to him.

'Mmm. Dart.' Hearing her whisper his name brought a new round of pleasure and pain. Pleasure because he knew she was now dreaming about him and pain because he knew they simply couldn't allow themselves to follow through on those dreams.

Tonight. He at least had tonight to capture her essence, to create a memory that would need to last him the rest of his life. Holding her. Feeling her hand on his chest. The rise and fall of her breaths, perfectly synchronised with his own. Her sweet, fresh scent encompassing him. *This* was what he would miss the most. The quietness of holding her in his arms, of protecting her, of keeping her safe.

Dart relaxed his body, knowing they had another hectic day tomorrow and that sleep was needed.

When he woke, it was to find the sun just starting to peek through the shadows of night. He shifted slightly, surprised and delighted to feel Emmy still in his arms, just starting to stir herself. He looked down at her, watching that first moment when she opened her eyes and saw him. The smile was on her face before those gorgeous baby blues opened and met his gaze. She stretched, their sleeping bags rubbing against each other as she angled her body closer to his.

'Good morning.' The smile was brighter now and within a second she'd leaned in and pressed a kiss to his lips. 'I slept so well.' As she said the words, she realised the complete truth of them. Not only was it the best sleep she'd had in a long time, she couldn't remember a time when she'd felt so secure, so protected. Being with Dart, in his arms, she'd known without a doubt that nothing bad would happen to her. Her subconscious must have known it as well because never before had she felt this refreshed first thing in the morning.

Dart was lying there, looking at her face as though she were the most precious thing in the world. It was an incredible feeling and one she wanted to continue for ever.

'You don't remember having a bad dream?' he asked, his voice thick and deep with relaxed slumber.

Emmy thought for a moment then shook her head. 'Nope.' Then she angled her head to the side. 'Did I?'

'Not a very long one. You wanted someone to leave you alone.'

'Oh.' Emmy's mouth went momentarily dry as she realised exactly what he was talking about. 'Sometimes I have small bad dreams.' She shrugged the thought away. 'It's nothing.'

'Did something happen to you when you were younger?'

She closed her eyes for a moment, not wanting to get into the kidnapping, which still gave her bad dreams every now and then. She'd probably had one last night because the soldiers with guns had triggered the memory. The strange thing was that she usually remembered the dreams, she usually woke up trembling and perspiring all over, gasping for air. That hadn't happened last night and she knew it was because she'd been held safe within Dart's arms, feeling as though nothing and no one would ever hurt her again.

She didn't want to think about that now. She wanted to concentrate on the incredible feeling she'd woken with, the one that Dart was responsible for creating. With him next to her, there would be no more bad dreams. There would be no more questions about whether someone could ever love her for herself rather than her fortune. Dartagnan Freeman had made an enormous impact in her life and she wanted him with her, to keep him in her life, by her side, holding her hand during the day and drawing her close at night.

'Yes, but I don't want to talk about that now,' she said as she leaned in for another kiss, disappointed that they couldn't enjoy a lovely, relaxing morning, taking their time with breakfast, sharing the paper and generally just spending time with each other. Not that she minded the alternative, being here in Tarparnii, helping out, learning so many new things, coping with busy medical clinics.

And she *had* coped. She was a good doctor.

She'd been able to treat her patients effectively and efficiently and she'd loved every moment of it. She was a good doctor and Dart thought so, too. What more could a girl want?

Resting her head onto his chest, she listened to the steady beating of his heart, loving the warmth of his arms about her, and even though the sun was starting to drive the temperature up, it was nothing compared to the way she felt when Dart held her. He could set her insides alight, make her entire body tingle with one of those smoulderingly deep looks he often sent her way. They may have only known each other for a few days but Emmy knew without a shadow of doubt that she was one hundred per cent, prime time, in love with him.

'I just want to absorb this moment in time. Just you and me.'

'And half of the PMA staff all squashed into one tent,' he pointed out as he reluctantly released her, knowing they needed to get the day under way. There was a lot of work still to be done today, a lot of patients to treat and distance to travel if they were going to return J'tagnan and his mother safely to their own village.

He leaned over and brushed a quick kiss on

Emmy's lips, delighting that she was allowing him to do so and also filing the sensations away in the back of his mind. He knew things would change the instant they returned to Australia.

There were several raised eyebrows between their colleagues when they realised that Dart and Emmy had become closer. It wasn't as though they flaunted the change but Emmy would trail her hand down his arm more slowly, more intimately than before. Or Dart would tuck a stray strand of hair behind her ear, smiling brightly. No one said anything, but smiled as they got on with the job they'd come here to do.

By midday, they were halfway through the clinic, Dart and Emmy barely finding two minutes together to sneak some alone time. Emmy couldn't believe how wonderful it was simply to be a doctor. Medicine was in her blood, it was what she had been called to do, and while her job at the television station allowed her to bring situations such as the one here in Tarparnii to the public's attention, she couldn't believe the satisfaction she felt at treating a patient, even if it was for an immunisation or just a check-up.

Around two o'clock, when there was a lull in patients, they all stopped for a bite to eat, Emmy taking a quick look at the digital footage her crew had shot. It looked good and she could already hear the commentary she would write and present play out in her head.

She felt rather than heard Dart come up behind her. 'How's it looking?' he asked as he slipped his hands about her waist.

'Good. The guys have shot some incredible stuff. It's going to be great.'

'No doubt.' He turned her in his arms so she was facing him, a smile bright on his lips as he bent to give her a quick kiss.

Emmy couldn't help but chuckle. 'You've certainly changed your tune since we first met. You didn't want to have anything to do with the filming.'

'Well, that was before I understood your vision. What you're doing here, Emmy, raising awareness of issues which are usually swept under the carpet, is good. Very good.' Dart was lowering his head, focusing on her luscious mouth, wanting nothing else than to taste the gloriousness which was his Emmy, when there was a loud shout from one of the villagers.

'Soldiers!'

At the one word, spoken in English, Emmy

froze to the spot. Soldiers? Here? Men with guns? She swallowed over the instant dryness of her throat, her eyes widening in fear.

'Where?' Dart called, releasing her and rushing over to the villager who had called the warning.

'Friend or foe?' Tarvon asked in his native tongue.

'Friend,' came the cry. 'Injured.'

Dart looked over at Emmy, surprised to see her standing right where he'd left her. It was exactly the way she'd looked when Weyakuu had been brought in the other day. 'Emmy?' He crossed quickly back to her side. 'Everything all right? You've gone pale.' Just as she had when they'd been in the truck, going through the checkpoint. Was she afraid of the soldiers? Or guns? He wouldn't blame her if she was but his gut told him there was more to it than that.

'Emmy?' Dart put his hand on her shoulder and she all but clamped onto his arm, drawing him close.

'I'll be fine in a moment,' she murmured as she breathed him in, trying to calm her racing fear.

'It's all right. The soldiers are friendly. Allies.'

'Will they still be carrying their guns? Weyakuu

didn't come into the village with a gun, just a bullet deep inside him from someone else's gun!'

'Em?' Dart was starting to get concerned. 'Are you sure you're going to be all right? If not, I can get Rick to assist me.'

Emmy breathed in one last breath, absorbing strength from him. 'I can do this.'

'Are you telling me or yourself?'

She eased back and nodded once. 'Both. Let's go see what the damage is.'

Together they walked over to where the injured soldier sat next to one of his friends, his rifle slung over his shoulder with a strap. Emmy reached over and grabbed Dart's hand, squeezing it a little.

Dart met her gaze. 'I won't let anything happen to you, Em,' he reassured her. 'Believe that.'

Emmy looked into his gorgeous brown eyes and then nodded, gaining strength from the man by her side. He *would* protect her.

'Status?' he asked Tarvon as they walked into the medical tent.

'Knife wound to the lower left leg. Bruises, scratches. Minor burn to the hand.

'Burn?' Dart asked as he stepped in for a closer

look, releasing Emmy's hand. 'Not a gunshot wound?' He looked to the solider and asked in Tarparnese, 'How did you get the burn?'

The soldier's answer made Dart's jaw clench. He straightened slowly.

'What did he say?' Emmy asked, picking up on the tension radiating from Dart.

'He said that a village not too far from here was under attack. Rebels came not too long ago, right through the village. Many are dead. A lot are injured. Just as these men were leaving to come here, one of the huts caught fire. He's not sure how. His hand got burnt from a hot ember.'

After finishing his explanation, Dart turned on his heel and stalked out of the tent to go and speak to the village headman. If another village was in trouble, they would need to provide whatever support they could. Such was the way of these people.

It didn't take long to gather a team together, Tarvon and a few other PMA personnel staying behind to provide any necessary medical treatment for those already headed here.

'The rest of us, grab whatever supplies you can and bring a bucket,' Dart said. 'We'll no doubt meet casualties along the route but if the fires aren't yet out, we'll need all the buckets we can find.' He turned to Emmy as everyone went off to get ready. 'I want you to stay here,' he said. 'Help Tarvon with any of the emergencies.'

'No. I'm coming with you. Tarvon has enough help.'

'Emmy. I need to know you're safe.'

'I *will* be safe and I'll also be by your side because that is the safest place for me.'

Dart's frustration instantly rose. 'I can't guarantee your safety when there's a jungle full of rebels and a village in need of attention.'

'I'm not asking for that type of protection, Dart. My crew and I will be there, filming and helping. That's what we've come here to do.'

'Ugh. Emmy.' He raked a hand through his hair. 'You are so frustrating at times. I can't concentrate properly if I know you're—'

'We're wasting time arguing,' she said, and started to head off, but he caught her arm, turning her to face him before pressing his mouth to hers, hard and furious.

'Promise me you'll stay safe. Promise me, Em,' he ground out, his voice laced with a need she'd never heard before. When she looked into his eyes, she couldn't believe the urgency reflected there. Urgency and...something else.

Emmy swallowed. 'I promise, but I'm still coming with you.'

He closed his eyes for a split second, as though accepting her resolve. 'You are so stubborn sometimes,' he murmured, before bringing his mouth to hers once more. After a few incredible seconds he put his arms on her shoulders and put her from him. 'Let's get ready.' He pushed all his emotional, irrational thoughts to the back of his mind. If he was going to be of any help to the villagers, to these wonderful Tarparniians, he needed to be one hundred per cent focused.

It wasn't too much longer until they were ready to leave, walking in a group towards the next village. If there were any rebels hiding in the leafy green scrub of the jungle, they weren't aware of them. Emmy walked beside Dart, feeling strong and empowered at the thought of helping these good people.

She'd been raised to be a figurehead, to listen and to help people. That hadn't been enough for her so she'd decided to study medicine. Even then, while she'd enjoyed helping people out in a more functional capacity, things still hadn't felt quite right. Going into the media had given her the opportunity to combine her philanthropic upbringing and her medical training.

Being here, though, walking through the jungles of Tarparnii, a backpack filled with supplies on her back and an empty wooden bucket in each hand, Emmy realised she was doing something she'd never really done before—she was giving with her heart. Here, she was able to use all of her skills *and* her deep-seated need to really help others. Here, she could make a massive difference and that was a powerful motivator, her mind already starting to whirl with different possibilities of how PMA could use more funds to help improve the life of the average Tarparniian.

It was a strange time to have such a revelation, just as she was about to walk into a potentially dangerous situation, but she wasn't scared, she wasn't worried. Looking up at Dart striding purposefully next to her enhanced her feelings and she couldn't believe how *right* everything felt.

As they neared the village, the smell of smoke filled the air and everyone quickened their pace. They'd met a few people along the way, either one or two of the PMA medics stopping to help or to encourage them to continue towards waiting medical help. When they came out into the village clearing, Emmy felt as though she'd stepped into an enormous accident scene.

There were people lying on the ground, crying; others were lying still, not moving. Women and children were huddled together, others were wailing. There was a long line of people creating a chain from the well in the centre of the village to the fire. It was chaos and for a split second Emmy had no idea where to help first. She didn't have to wonder long as Dart started calling instructions.

'Emmy, work triage with Gloria. Rick and Sue, first aid. Set up tables, and use the supplies sparingly because they're all we've got. If any patients can be sent through to Tarvon, send them on their way. The fewer people we have milling around, the better.' Dart then went forward with the rest of the village men, walking into the fray. Even though it was the middle of the day, the smoke had turned the area dark and inhospitable.

Emmy couldn't help but watch him go, her heart pounding with a mixture of apprehension and adrenalin, the smell of smoke filling her senses. Work. Job. Professional. She and the others took off their packs, offered their empty buckets for the villagers to use and started to assess their patients. Emmy glanced over towards the well and could just make out Dart's tall, powerful frame as he talked to one of the village elders as they filled buckets with water.

A loud cry, a scream of anguish, rang out into the air and Emmy's heart almost stopped beating. What was that? She must have spoken out loud as Gloria translated.

'Someone is asking for help. They can't find their child.'

Emmy swallowed, her throat dry. 'How old is the child?'

Gloria listened for a moment as she and Emmy continued bandaging up a burn on a man's arm. 'Er…about five.'

'Wait here,' she said, and ignoring other cries headed towards Dart. Another loud cry went up and a woman was pointing towards the hut that was on fire, her words rapid and urgent.

'*QaH! QaH!*' the woman called, pointing urgently. Emmy had heard that word enough during her time here. It meant 'help'.

Then, before she could call out to Dart, ask him what was going on, she watched in horror as he took off, heading directly towards the building that was ablaze.

'*No!*' The word was wrenched from her and as though in slow motion she saw Dart drape himself with a wet blanket and head into the heat. She took a few steps after him but was restrained by one of the men. She turned. 'What's he doing? Where's he going?'

'A child. Trapped,' the village headman said. 'Dart rescue.'

Emmy couldn't believe it. Dart might die. No. She couldn't even begin to think like that and as Gloria called for her, Emmy couldn't believe how torn she was. She wanted to stand there and wait for Dart, to make sure he came out, that he was OK, but at the same time she had a job to do.

'Emmy.' There was urgency in Gloria's tone. 'This woman's baby's head is crowning.'

'What?' Emmy clenched her teeth, turned away from the burning building and stalked back to where Gloria was madly trying to prepare for an impromptu birth.

'The baby's small. The woman said she has another moon cycle to go before the baby is ready.'

'Is this her first?' Emmy pulled on a pair of

gloves and crouched down on the grass beside the birthing mother. Gloria asked the question.

'No. It's her fifth.'

'It's going to be quick,' she murmured as she felt the top of the baby's head. The birthing woman was panting and moaning, saying a lot of words. 'Translate, please?'

'She says she doesn't want this to happen,' Gloria said as she did the mother's observations. 'She says she does not have her daughters and cousins around her, that there should not be men near.'

'The head is out,' Emmy announced, then looked at Gloria, thinking quickly. 'Tell her we are sorry and respect her customs but this baby is eager to meet her, wants to be held in her arms and suckled at her breast.'

Gloria nodded and translated quickly. The woman moaned and groaned again, pushing hard as the next contraction came.

'You're doing an excellent job,' Emmy praised, working hard to keep her mind focused even though her stomach was in knots with fear for Dart. Had he come out? Had he found the child? Was he all right? 'Shoulders have rotated,' she announced. 'Gloria, this is going to be quick. Do we have forceps? String? Something to tie the umbilical cord with?'

Gloria shifted around to crouch next to Emmy and produced a clean sheet, locking forceps and scissors. 'Everything you need, Doctor.'

As Emmy had predicted, within the next few contractions the baby was born, four weeks early but with a healthy set of lungs, the impatient cries filling the night. 'A baby boy,' she said, and after Gloria had assisted her in clamping and cutting the cord, she loosely wrapped the baby and placed him in his mother's arms. Gloria translated her words as she continued to speak to the mother. 'He was born on a night when the men needed help. He will be a strong man, a man who will always help,' she told the mother with a smile.

The mother grasped her new babe to her and just as quickly put him to the breast, where he started to feed. After they delivered the afterbirth, Emmy left the new mother in Gloria's capable hands and pulled off her gloves.

'Nicely done,' a deep voice said from behind her, and Emmy spun around so fast she almost cricked her neck.

'Dart!' She stared at him, quite unable to believe he was before her, but a second later she put her hands around his neck and brought his mouth to hers. 'You're OK. You're fine.'

'Yes. Was that the first baby you've delivered, Dr Jofille?'

'Yes. What about the boy? Did you find him? Was he—?'

Dart raised a tired arm and pointed to where a woman was cradling her child, Sue making sure both mother and son were fine. 'Smoke inhalation. He'll be fine. Wanted to prove to his brothers that he *was* old enough to help put the fire out.' Dart turned his attention back to look at Emerson. 'And you? Delivering a baby. Taking the lead in a medical emergency like you've been in Tarparnii for years.'

She dropped her hands and waved away his words. 'I'm more concerned about you. Did *you* suffer smoke inhalation?' she asked.

'I'm fine.'

'Dart.' Her voice changed to one of annoyed concern. 'You could have been killed.'

'Nah.' There was a smile in his voice.

'Don't you go all cute and gorgeous on me, Dartagnan Freeman. I'm very cross.' As she spoke, Emmy could feel a shift in the breeze, the air around them starting to cool very slightly.

Dart looked up and smiled. 'Weather's changing.' He couldn't believe how exhausted he felt. The flames from the fire had been so hot that his eyes had stung as he'd looked for the young boy.

'Don't change the subject. Why did you go in? Don't you know it's dangerous to go into a burning building?'

'I knew what I was doing, Emmy.' His tone had tightened a little. 'It's not the first time I've had to run into a burning building.'

She stopped, her anger dissipating quickly. 'Oh?'

'I wasn't going to lose that little boy to those flames. Or myself, for that matter. I've already lost far too many people in circumstances like this and I wasn't going to lose anyone else.'

And there it was. The words were almost choked from his mouth, as though his throat was not only constricting from the smoke but also because he'd lost people he'd loved to fire. His parents? Someone else? Someone very important to him. She recalled Meeree saying that Dart was alone, had a large void of loneliness in his life, and while his giving might cover over the hole, it didn't fill it.

Could she fill it? Was there the possibility that this love she felt for him could turn into something more? She wasn't naïve enough to think that simply because she loved Dart their lives would end happily ever after. She knew, after her upbringing, that even if someone said they loved you, it didn't necessarily mean that things would turn out right.

As she looked at him, trying to figure out what to say next without sounding as though she was prying into his past, the first few raindrops fell onto the top of her head. She didn't move, her gaze still fixed on Dart's.

A loud cheer went up as the rain continued to fall in its usual steady rhythm. The people around them were hugging and clapping and cheering and laughing, their dark-skinned faces beaming brightly. The rain had come. The rain would help put out the fire. They were saved.

'We'd better finish treating these people and get back to the village. The rain will take care of the fire.'

Just like that, he shut her out. It was as though he'd slammed a door in her face and Emmy visibly winced.

CHAPTER ELEVEN

FOR the rest of the day, they attended to a few people who required medical treatment. Afterwards, they changed their clothes, had something to eat and packed up their things, ready to head to the next village—J'tagnan's village.

Throughout it all Emmy tried to behave as normally as she could. She'd become an expert at hiding her true feelings—from everyone—in the past and she had hoped that Dart was the one person she *wouldn't* need to hide them from, that around him she could be one hundred per cent herself. Apparently not.

On the truck, as they headed to the next village, he made a point of sitting next to her. His attitude only made Emmy even more confused than she'd been before. It was as though he'd pigeonholed what had happened after the fire. She felt he'd been on the brink of opening up to her, of telling her about his past, when he'd clammed up tight.

When the truck started to slow, Emmy looked

out at the scenery, noticing that they were still on the main track. She'd learned by now that the villages were all tucked away in the countryside, away from the main thoroughfares, near the streams and waterholes where water could be provided. The slowing down of the truck probably meant another checkpoint. She swallowed, her throat instantly going dry because she knew that a checkpoint meant soldiers with guns.

'Are you OK?' Dart asked, turning to look at her.

'What? Uh… I'm fine.' She forced a smile but even she could tell she wasn't selling it. Not to him. Not now that they'd spent so much time together.

'Emmy, you're squeezing my hand.' His free hand reached out to turn her chin so she was facing him, concern instantly marring his brow. 'And you've gone pale. What's wrong, Em?'

The truck had almost come to a stop and her breathing had increased slightly, even though she was trying to control it.

'Guns.' She pursed her lips together and shrugged quickly, swallowing again, her mouth still dry. 'I have a…a…thing about guns.'

Dart continued to stare deeply into her eyes for

another long moment and she wondered just what he saw. 'Something happened to you. Long ago,' he murmured as the truck's brakes brought the vehicle to a halt. He nodded then leaned forward and pressed a firm but reassuring kiss to her lips. 'Don't you worry, Emmy. I'll protect you.' His words were direct, forceful and she believed him, one hundred per cent.

Slowly she let go of the large breath she hadn't even realised she'd been holding and forced herself to relax. 'OK,' she whispered, believing every word he spoke.

'Good.' His smile was small and he squeezed her hand reassuringly. 'Now, I need your papers. I'll only be gone for a minute or two and then I'll be right back here, by your side. Understand?'

She nodded and swallowed again, feeling the dryness beginning to fade. Dart was here. Dart would protect her. This time, as she watched him move away from her and jump off the back of the truck, along with Tarvon, she didn't feel so worried about him. He was a strong, capable man. The man she loved with all her heart.

With no fuss at all, they were cleared through the checkpoint, Dart coming to sit back down beside her.

'How are you feeling now?' he asked as he took her hand in his.

'Better.'

Dart leaned closer and spoke softly near her ear.

'Something happened in your past, didn't it?'

'How can you tell?' she asked, her confused and concerned eyes looking into his sure and steady ones.

'Wealthy family plus guns. Not a usual combination except in the form of a kidnapping.'

Emmy gasped at his words and Dart watched as the colour drained from her face.

'How old were you?'

'Five.' The one word was barely audible but Dart could hear her. Even over the rumble of the trucks and the noises from the rest of the people in the transport he could hear her and he realised it was because his heart was joined with hers. Emmy had become a part of him, a part of his vision, a part of his sense of smell, a part of his hearing, his speech. Her hand started trembling in his but he had one arm around her, holding her close, before it could take hold.

'Oh, Emmy.' He couldn't even begin to imagine what she'd gone through. Kidnapped at five years of age! No wonder she didn't like guns. He eased her back slightly. 'Did they hurt you? Were you…?'

'No. I was only taken for twenty-four hours. My father quickly agreed to pay the ransom. I had one night away from my parents and I was drugged for most of it so I don't remember a lot.'

Dart closed his eyes against the heartbreak he felt for her younger self. The poor child. Confused. Disoriented. Scared beyond belief. 'How did they get to you?'

Emmy let out a slow breath and eased back from his hold, still making sure he could hear her properly. 'OK, I'll say this quickly. I was being driven to school. Patrick, my driver, stopped the car for some reason and all I remember was him getting out and a man climbing into the back of the car. He had a mask over his face and a gun in his hand. Another man climbed into the driver's seat and then… I…I… Everything after that is blurry.'

She sucked in a deep breath and let it out slowly. 'My father paid the money. A private investigator who my father kept on retainer found me and brought me home. My nanny was beside herself. Crying. Welcoming me with opened arms.

Patrick, my driver, was in the hospital. I remember Nanny taking me to visit him. My parents...' Emmy stopped, her eyes stinging with tears, her throat closing up.

She bit her lip to try and control her emotions as she breathed in and out again, knowing she had to share this devastating part of her life with Dart if there was ever any possibility of a future for them. 'They...uh...weren't even there when I came home. Doctors came to check me out, to make sure I was all right. I saw my father two days later. He told me it was *unfortunate* what had happened but that he'd laid aside a sum of money specifically for such purposes for both my brother and myself.'

She shook her head and shrugged, an angry lone tear sliding down her cheek. 'No hug. No reassurance for a scared little girl. My mother and I have never spoken of it. It was just another one of those things that was pushed aside as not important. I'd been kidnapped. They'd paid the money. I'd been returned. End of story.'

Dart was horrified. 'But the police?'

'Were never involved. As far as I know, the kidnappers were never brought to justice but after that I was ripped from the school that I'd loved so much and sent to a boarding school that had twenty-four-hour security.'

'But…you were *five*.'

'And a nuisance to my parents. For years I believed that being kidnapped was my fault, that I was punished for it.'

Dart raked a hand through his hair, his heart bleeding for the small child and the pain and confusion she must have felt. 'How long were you at boarding school?'

'Until I'd finished. The only times I saw my mother was when she took me to luncheons or functions so I could learn to be a proper young lady. Deportment, elocution and etiquette until I turned eighteen. By then I'd realised I needed more…more than fine-art exhibitions or museum openings.

'I had Liam, my personal bodyguard, teach me self-defence, and learning those skills helped me far more than the years of therapy my parents forced me to attend. They gave me deep confidence as well as a belief in myself. I already knew which fork to use and when. I knew how to make polite conversation with heads of state and I was almost suffocating in the box my parents had stuffed me into, and all because some greedy kidnapper thought it was OK to steal me.' Emmy ground out the last few words, unable to believe the anger she felt, not only towards her parents but towards the kidnapper and just how much that incident had shaped the rest of her life.

'You've called me a poor little rich girl, Dart.' She laughed without humour. 'You have no idea just how right you were.'

'Emmy, I didn't realise everything you'd been through.' His admiration for the woman increased rapidly. 'You're so strong, so encompassing, so sure of yourself.' The trucks were turning off now, taking a rougher road as they headed for the next village. Neither Dart nor Emmy noticed.

'Sure of myself?' Emmy shook her head. 'Hardly.'

'But you are. You see something you want and you don't hold back, you go for it. You wanted to go to medical school and you went. You wanted to come to Tarparnii and here you are.'

'I'm not as confident as I make out.'

'I disagree.'

Emmy closed her eyes tightly for a moment before opening them and saying the words that were in her heart. 'I'm not strong, Dart. Although I received good grades in med school, I was never sure whether I'd earned them or been awarded the marks. It wasn't until today when I was able to deliver that baby all by myself that I finally realised that I *am* a good doctor.'

'You are, Em. You're a very good doctor.'

'But then, when it started to rain, you…shut me out. I'm not strong enough to break down your walls, Dart. I'm more than willing to listen to anything you have to say, to support you, to be there for you because I…I…' She stopped and took a calming breath before whispering softly, 'I love you.'

Dart stared at her. The trucks slowed down and finally came to a halt. He didn't speak and Emmy closed her eyes, knowing she'd made a mistake in telling him of her true feelings. The other personnel in the truck instantly started to move but Dart stayed where he was, staring into Emmy's gorgeous blue eyes, eyes that were now filled with confusion and doubt.

'What?' he prompted as though he hadn't heard her properly.

She shook her head. 'It doesn't matter now. We're here.'

'We'll let the others go first.'

Now that the engine had stopped, there was less

of a bubble surrounding them as people shifted past them, starting to heft the medical boxes out of the truck. She felt highly self-conscious, biting her lip and wishing she'd kept her mouth shut.

'Emmy,' he said when it was just the two of them left in the truck. 'Are you sure? I know that might sound like an odd question given what you've just declared but—'

'You probably think that I don't know what I'm feeling, that I'm simply infatuated with you,' she interjected, not wanting to have this conversation but wanting him to realise that she *did* know her own mind. 'That because we're out in the jungle, away from the usual trappings of my life, that once we get back to Australia, I'll realise what I feel for you isn't really real.'

'I've seen it happen too many times,' Dart defended softly, feeling like an absolute heel for not being able to respond the way she would have hoped. 'People come here. They work in close, isolated situations and bonds start to form, relationships grow and before you know it, they're ready to commit to a lifetime together that nothing will ever tear apart. Then they return home and within weeks of getting back they realise their mistake and go their separate ways. It happens all the time.'

'And so you just presume that I'm like that?' She was stung by his words, realising that he was trying to let her down gently. 'That a woman who has only ever been loved by her domestic employees wouldn't know what real love is so therefore how can she profess, after only a few days, to being in love with you? That I have no depth of feeling? That I don't long, with all my heart, for you to say those words back to me? That I am so shallow?'

Emmy shifted from his arms and stood as she continued speaking. 'I love you, Dart. Nothing you say or do is ever going to change that. This is a forever love and I know that because I have *never* felt this way about anyone.' Emmy shoved her hands into the pockets of her designer jeans and without another word stepped from the truck, heading over to help the others, far away from him.

He made his way into the village. The welcoming ceremony for baby J'tagnan was already under way, the babe being held high in the air by the village elder for all to see. Women were placing leis over the mother's head, welcoming her back to their home and praising her for the good work in bringing another strong male into their community. There was much cheering, clapping and whooping. Everyone was very happy.

Except Emmy.

Dart watched her as she stood near her crew, clapping along, but he could tell she wasn't really enjoying the festivities and he knew that was his fault. He should go to her, tell her that she meant a great deal to him but he knew she wouldn't feel the same way once they were back home.

Still, he owed her an apology. Her feelings were her own and if she chose to give them or share them, he still had to respect that. The fact that she meant a lot to him was evident by the way he didn't seem able to keep his hands to himself. Since he'd met her, the large void he'd carried in his life for the past six years hadn't seemed as painful. That much he freely acknowledged and he needed to ensure his lack of appropriate response to her declaration hadn't hurt the woman who meant a great deal to him.

As he headed towards Emmy, he was stopped by several of the villagers, holding his hands in theirs in a form of welcome and thanks. The Tarparniians were quiet, proud people but they knew that it was Dart who had taken care of J'tagnan and his mother, ensuring that neither had died.

He accepted their thanks, he smiled and spoke quietly as he slowly made his way towards where Emmy was standing, only to find when he reached her crew that she'd disappeared. Dart frantically searched the area for her but unsuccessfully. Where had she gone?

Tarvon was standing near the film crew and noticed Dart's face. 'She's over there,' he said with a large smile as he pointed to a clearing in the lush green trees. Dart saw Emmy, her back straight and proud, walking away from him.

'Thanks,' he murmured, and quickly headed in her direction, his earlier hesitancy disappearing in his need to catch her. 'Emmy?' he called, but either she didn't hear him over the noise of the celebration or she was ignoring him. His heart leapt into his throat. Was he too late to apologise? Had he made her too mad?

'Emerson,' he called again, a little louder, his long strides helping him to catch up to her, closing the distance between them. This time she stopped and turned and Dart could see the tears glistening in her eyes. Guilt instantly racked him because he knew he was responsible for making her upset.

He half expected her to square her shoulders, gently brush away the tears, lift her chin, her posture perfect, as he'd already seen her do several times. But she didn't.

'What now, Dart?' Even more tears welled in her eyes as she looked up at him. She blinked once, twice, her vision blurring, her lashes wet with the tears that were now overflowing onto her cheeks. 'Do you need more evidence of my feelings? To know that even with all my debutante and finishing-school training, I still can't pull myself together enough to be around for J'tagnan's happy homecoming? I hate feeling out of control and *you've* made me feel this way. You've brushed my feelings aside, content just to hold my hand, to kiss me, to say that you'll protect me, when in actual fact you're only planning on doing those things until we leave Tarparnii.'

She worked hard to keep her voice strong, to get the words out that she needed to say. So many times in the past, in so many different circumstances, she'd bitten her tongue, she'd held the words back, she'd been the perfect hostess, always polite, never emotional. Well, not this time.

'I love you, Dart. I *love* you, and if you don't want that love, fine. You don't have to have it but it also means that from this point onwards you don't have *any* of me. I will not be some toy, some pawn you use. I've been used enough. I've been pushed and pulled in one direction or another my entire life and I've decided that enough is enough.'

'And you don't think you're a strong woman,' he stated clearly.

She brushed impatiently at the tears before spreading her arms wide. 'I don't feel strong. I'm standing here. Crying in front of you. Begging for affection.' She shook her head again. 'Why is it that I always have to beg for affection? Why am I always the one who is doing the chasing, especially when I never end up catching anything but indifference?' She hiccupped a few times before covering her face with her hands. 'I'm a fool. That's what I am.'

'You're not a fool.' His words were vehement. 'You are *not* a fool, Emmy. You're incredible. You're wonderful. You're powerful, and I'm sorry.'

'Sorry?'

'For not believing you meant every word you've ever said to me.'

'So…you believe that I love you?'

'Yes.'

'That it's not just an infatuation? That it's not just a holiday fling?'

He paused. 'Your feelings are yours. I should never have discounted them.' Dart wanted to haul her into his arms, to wipe away her tears, to press his mouth to hers and never let her go. 'I couldn't allow myself to believe that you loved me because I didn't think I deserved it.'

'Deserved…?' Emmy was slightly confused and removed her hands from her face, accepting the tissue he held out to her.

'Your love. I didn't think I deserved a second chance at happiness and made myself believe that what you felt for me was only a passing infatuation. That it wouldn't last.'

'*Second* chance? So you have lost someone dear to you.'

Dart nodded. It was time. Time to open up the past and share it with this special woman. 'Six years ago. A raging bush fire ripped through the countryside where my parents lived. It tore the place apart, the flames huge, like a towering inferno. I'd gone home for Christmas, taking my…my fiancée with me.'

Emmy had a quick mind and she realised in an instant what Dart was saying. His parents. Family and friends and…his *fiancée*. He'd lost too many people, maybe the three people he'd cared about most, in one of the most horrific fires their country had ever seen. She remembered the fires. She remembered seeing pictures of the devastation. She'd been working overseas in England at the time but it hadn't stopped her from sympathising with the plight of her countrymen. Now she discovered that the man she loved had lost those who had been most dear to him in those very fires.

'Oh, Dart.' Emmy put her hands on either side of his face and kissed him. His arms came instantly around her, holding her close, grateful for her touch.

'That's why I couldn't lose you. I needed to know you were safe,' he murmured, kissing her soundly. 'You've come to mean so much to me in such a short time, Emmy. For years I've carried around the loss of Marta and my parents. They left an enormous void in my heart, one I thought would never be filled. I've lived with my loneliness, wishing I'd been able to do more, wishing I'd been there with them at the end, but I wasn't. I'd been called back to the city for a couple of days. They were fleeing the fires, driving away from the danger...but they weren't quick enough.' He broke off and pulled back from her, still holding her hands in his.

'In one brief, devastating moment I lost everyone I loved. It left an enormous hole inside me. For a long time I had no idea how to cope with my loneliness, the guilt I felt, even though I know there was nothing I could have done to help them. I've come here to Tarparnii ever since and I have to say that being here, helping these people, it does go a long way to helping ease my pain.'

'But it never completely goes away,' she stated.

'Correct.'

'Dart.' She looked into his eyes. 'I know that feeling. The one where you're surrounded by people but still feel so hollow, so alone deep down inside.'

Dart remembered how she'd told him about her family life, how she'd been raised in a household devoid of love. Yes, she understood that feeling of loneliness and even though they'd walked very different paths, they'd ended up at the same place. Perhaps it had been inevitable that they meet. It was as though their lives had taken different twists and turns but both of them had ended up here, at this moment in time, together in each other's arms.

'I'm sorry you've had so much pain in your life,' he murmured, drawing her closer again.

'The pain isn't that bad any more.'

'Something changed?' he asked, a small smile on his lips.

'Yes. You. You've come into my life and splashed it with bright, beautiful colours, Dartagnan Freeman, and I can't thank you enough for everything you've done for me.' She smiled through the silent tears that had slid down her face at hearing him talk of his past.

'I haven't done anything except perhaps help you realise your own inner strength.'

She smiled and sighed, resting her head on his shoulder. She knew he hadn't confessed to loving her but he *had* opened up about his past, he'd shared his pain with her, and that in itself told her she was important to him.

After a few minutes of standing in silence, she eased back and took his hand in hers. 'Let's go back to the celebrations.' Dart smiled and hand in hand they walked back towards the gathering, Emmy felt strong and secure, not only in her self but in her ability to convince Dart that the emotions that existed between them were destined to last a lifetime.

CHAPTER TWELVE

WHEN Emmy looked out of the small window of the aircraft, the early morning sunrise having been one of the best she'd seen in a long time, she couldn't help her excitement at seeing Sydney airport below. While she'd had a great time in Tarparnii, she was also happy to return, eager not only to get to the studio to start editing the film footage but also to be back in her own country... with Dart at her side.

During the past few days they'd worked alongside each other in clinics, they'd pitched tents, lugged medical supplies to and from the trucks. On the way back to Meeree and Jalak's village, Dart had encouraged Emmy to climb from the truck and meet the young soldiers who were only doing their duty.

Emmy had been highly resistant at first but with his careful encouragement and the promise that he'd keep very close to her at all times, she was able to see that the young men with guns were only doing their job and were quite nice to talk to. She knew it was nothing like her previous experience with guns and the horrifying kidnapping she'd endured, but it was still one step closer to helping her get rid of the sporadic nightmares that had plagued her dreams ever since the event.

Having Dart by her side had made her feel safe, protected, and she knew she wanted to feel that way for the rest of her life. She wanted him with her, needed him with her, and she certainly hoped he felt the same way.

Although ever since they'd said farewell to Meeree and Jalak, Dart had seemed to grow rather pensive and now, as she held his hand, her excitement bubbling over at arriving back in Australia, he seemed agitated and unsettled within himself. Why wasn't he excited about coming home? He had three days in Sydney for a debrief with PMA before he would head home to Brisbane, where he lived.

Emmy angled her head to the side and looked at him. Was that the problem? Did he think that because they lived in different States a little thing like geography would keep them apart? Was he still worried that now they were out of the tense and very different situations they'd faced in

Tarparnii, they would change? Drift apart? He believed she loved him, of that she was certain, but was he being cautious because things could still go wrong? She wished he'd talk to her rather than retreating within himself.

'An uneventful flight,' she murmured as they disembarked from the small plane and walked into Sydney airport, Dart still quiet but his arm firmly around her shoulders. 'Do you have to go straight to PMA?' she asked.

'Yes.'

Emmy nodded. 'I'll be heading to the studio with my crew. Shall we meet later?'

'OK.'

She tried not to grit her teeth at his monosyllabic answers and it reminded her of the first day they'd met. Hadn't they both changed? Taken a step forward into a new part of their lives? She knew she'd decided to wait for him to get his head around things but it didn't mean she wasn't going to get totally frustrated with him. 'Great.' She worked hard to keep her tone upbeat. 'When? Where?'

Dart stopped walking and looked at her. They were in the main baggage claim area, and the place was swarming with people. There were chauffeurs holding cards with names scribbled on them, there were families hugging and greeting each other, talking non-stop to catch up on news. There were photographers, journalists, television crews and reporters swarming around someone at the far end. There were businessmen, walking out of the airport doors, briefcases in one hand, overnight bags in the other. There were so many people and where, usually in crowds like this, he'd felt isolated and alone, making his way through everyone else's hustle and bustle, this time, with Emmy by his side, holding his hand, talking to him, the loneliness had disappeared.

Dart knew he should get his head together and as he looked at her now, hearing the veiled frustration in her tone, he realised he should actually pay her some attention, talk to her, open up to her.

He simply wasn't used to it. For far too long it had been he and his thoughts, alone together. Alone… He didn't want to be alone again. He had Emmy and in the past few days she'd shown him what life could be like once that enormous, lonely void he'd been living with for the past six years was filled.

'Sorry, Em.' They'd stopped by the baggage

carousel so that Emmy and her crew could collect their bags and equipment. Dart put down his one canvas bag and cupped her face in his hands, bending down to brush a kiss across her lips. 'I haven't been very good company for the past few hours.'

'No.' She smiled, pleased he was talking to her. 'Why is that, do you think?' And please don't tell me it's because you're having second thoughts about us, she thought silently. While nothing clear had been resolved about their futures, the fact that they were interested in spending time together was what she was working with.

'I feel…disjointed whenever I return to Australia. It's just how things have always been ever since I joined PMA six years ago.' He closed his eyes for a moment as though trying to think of the most straightforward way to explain how he felt.

'Going to Tarparnii offered me an escape from my life here and in some ways I guess I prefer my life in a jungle in the middle of nowhere rather than here, in a large city in the middle of everyone.' He glanced around at the people near them. One or two guys with cameras around their necks were talking to Emmy's crew; families were embracing and others were hefting luggage off the carousel, eager to be outside.

He returned his focus to the woman who held his heart. 'Besides, I've never had anyone here when I arrived back in the country. After my parents and Marta...' He stopped and shook his head. The past was the past. He needed to think forward into the future, even though he had no idea what that held. 'I've never had anyone special to greet me. Also, I don't particularly like airports. Always so busy.'

Emmy giggled. 'They do tend to be that way, yes.'

At her teasing words, her laughter, he looked down into those blue eyes he could continue looking into all day, every day, for the rest of his life. 'Now, though...now I have you.'

'Yes, you do.'

He exhaled slowly, feeling the previous tension and stress melt away. 'You are so incredibly beautiful, my Emerson-Rose. Your eyes are like the sky on a cloudless day, so bright, so blue and so relaxing.'

Her lips curved up into a wide smile before she grabbed at the front of his polo shirt and tugged his head towards hers. 'You really shouldn't say things like that to me because then I can't resist kissing you,' she whispered against his mouth.

'Ah…but maybe I say things like that simply so you *will* kiss me.'

'Smart man.' With that, she stood on tiptoe, desperate to close the remaining distance between them, desperate for his mouth to be on hers, making her feel as though she were the most precious, most gorgeous woman in the world. She loved the way his arms came about her, making her feel so loved, so protected.

He'd been lost and lonely for so long that his own country felt foreign to him. Flashes of white light surrounded them and it was as though the rest of the airport patrons disappeared. She knew it was often this way when Dart held her, when he kissed her, when he let her feel just how important she was to him. Nothing mattered except for the two of them.

With incredible reluctance he drew back, knowing this venue was not the place to start something they had no time to finish. Dart kissed her once more. 'I need to get going. Where do you want to meet tonight?'

Emmy smiled, a plan forming in her mind. 'You haven't seen much of Sydney, have you?'

He shook his head. 'It's usually just a stop-over between Brisbane and Tarparnii and only then because PMA headquarters is here.'

'Well, tonight, my darling Dartagnan, I am going to show you *my* Sydney. I'll send a car to pick you up from your Parramatta hotel at seven o'clock. Make sure you're ready.'

She'd send a car? Dart dismissed the thought, not wanting to be the cause of making the light in her eyes disappear. She was happy. His Emmy was happy. Surely that was all that mattered? 'All right.' He bent and claimed her luscious lips once more, still marvelling at the fact that he had the right to do so even though they came from very different worlds.

Case in point—she was going to send a car for him. Why couldn't he simply catch a taxi and meet her? He knew she had a town-house in Sydney and he knew it was in one of the expensive suburbs, close to the Harbour Bridge and the Opera House. Dart had also expected her to suggest he come and stay with her while he was in town but she hadn't. Did that mean that she didn't want him to see her place? That she thought he might think it was too fancy? Too flashy? Too rich?

He pushed the thoughts from his mind, simply content at this moment just to absorb her, hold her close, taste her sweet goodness, which he knew would only leave him begging for more.

'Will you two get a room?' Emmy heard her cameraman mutter. 'You're making me miss my wife.'

They broke apart, Emmy smiling at her colleague before reluctantly releasing the man of her dreams. 'Until tonight.' She held his hand as they stretched apart, Dart slowly moving away from her. When only their fingertips were touching, Emmy started to feel a sense of panic. She didn't want him to go. She wanted him to stay, never leave her side, always be with her, but she knew neither of them could live the rest of their lives in each other's pockets. That wasn't how happy and healthy relationships progressed.

She'd worked long and hard to gain her independence and she knew that Dart would never take it away from her. Rather, he would be there, strengthening her, encouraging her, helping her to reach her full potential.

Dart gave her fingers a little squeeze then winked as he let go. 'Tonight.'

As Emmy watched him walk away from her,

she felt bereft, as though a part of her was instantly missing... And it was.

Dart opened the door to the room at the modest hotel at a quarter to seven, feeling exhausted from the day of being poked and prodded by the PMA medics to ensure he was in good health. He'd had a psychological evaluation and would undergo another one tomorrow. He'd handed in paperwork and passed on his appraisal of Tarvon. Combined with the emotional upheaval of leaving Meeree and Jalak, his other friends with PMA and Tarparnii in general, it had been a very full day.

Yet throughout the entire day, he'd felt as though a part of him had been missing. He'd found himself on several occasions looking around for Emerson, expecting her to be somewhere close. It had taken a split second for him to realise he was doing this and each time his pain at being separated from her increased.

It was an odd sensation to be so reliant on someone else when for so long he'd locked his heart away. He had no idea how things were going to work out with Emmy. He wasn't locked into working in Brisbane but wasn't sure he wanted to move to Sydney. The logistics, the necessity to make plans had given him a headache so he'd vowed not to think about them...for now.

As he stood beneath the hot, refreshing spray of the shower he knew the last thing he wanted to do was to go out. Why couldn't Emmy just come here? They could snuggle up together, watch a movie and order some room service. Then he remembered the way her eyes had come alive at the thought of being out in Sydney with him, of showing him the city she lived in, and he knew he would never be able to refuse her such an experience.

He'd just finished dressing, wearing a pair of jeans, shoes and a clean polo shirt, when there was a knock at the door. That would no doubt be the driver of the car Emmy had sent for him. He reached for his wallet and room key before opening the door, surprised to find a hotel employee standing there.

'Oh, good evening, Dr Freeman.' The slightly balding man in an off-the-rack suit held out his hand. 'I'm Mr Pfeiffer, the hotel's manager.'

'Is there a problem?'

'Uh...no. No. I simply wanted let you know that the car is here to pick you up and has been redirected to the rear of the premises. I'd be happy to escort you.'

Dart frowned as he closed the door and stepped out into the corridor. 'Why is the car out the back?'

'Because of the press in the front lobby, sir.'

'Press?' Dart's eyebrows hit his hairline.

'Yes, sir.' Mr Pfeiffer held out an evening paper. Dart's eyes almost bulged out of his head as he saw a picture of Emerson and himself kissing passionately at the airport. The picture was on the front page with a large splashy caption that read, Emmy's Mystery Man—Love at Last?

'But…this was only this morning.' Dart was completely perplexed. He had no idea how he could be on the front cover of a newspaper so quickly.

'The paparazzi work fast,' the hotel manager replied. 'This way, if you please, Dr Freeman.'

'How did they find me? None of this makes any sense.' Dart allowed himself to be led through the hotel to the rear doors where a limousine was waiting, the chauffeur opening the door the instant he saw Dart.

'Please feel free to use this entrance on your return if necessary, Dr Freeman,' Mr Pfeiffer said, simpering, and as Dart glanced back at the man, he couldn't help but notice how the hotel manager's eyes gleamed with delight. No doubt it was a coup for him to have such an important guest staying in his hotel.

Dart shook his head in astonishment and quickly climbed into the rear of the limo, pleased, surprised and relieved to find Emmy waiting for him inside. She was dressed in a dark blue dress, her hair curled and coiled on top of her head, light make-up highlighting her incredible features. Her smile was bright and encompassing and the instant he sat down she reached for him, drawing him close and pressing her mouth to his.

'You look…' Very different, he wanted to say, but he couldn't help the way his body responded to the way she was dressed. 'Beautiful, Emmy. You always do. No matter what you're wearing.'

She laughed and the sound did something to ease his frazzled mind. 'I've missed you so much today. I had no idea it would be this much,' she murmured against his lips. 'After being together night and day, especially for the past few days, it's been so strange not to be with you,' she continued as the car started to move.

Dart was still stunned, not sure what to say to

Emmy, not sure what to do about the fact that he was on the front cover of a newspaper. He edged back from her embrace and removed her hands from his face, putting them into her lap.

It was the first inkling she had that something was wrong. 'Dart?'

Without a word he placed the paper in her hands. Emmy looked down at it then sighed. 'It didn't take them long, did it?' She met his gaze. 'I guess we might need to learn to be a bit more discreet.'

Dart blinked. 'Discreet?' He paused for a moment then asked, 'Aren't you concerned about this?'

'Dart, it's hardly the first time I've been in the news. You know that.'

'I do but…it's the first time for me and I don't remember saying that a paper can print my picture willy-nilly.'

Emmy opened the paper and flicked past the local news until she came to a double-page spread of the two of them kissing at the airport, a photograph of them, arms around each other, unable to let go of each other.

'There's *more*?'

Emmy closed her eyes at the anger and censure

she heard in his tone. 'I understand how this might be upsetting to you but it will all blow over. It's just because it's new and because I've never been photographed…kissing…anyone… like that before.'

'I'm in a newspaper!' The incredulity in his tone almost made her smile and her heart went out to him.

'It's a different world, Dart. I know that. We'll be a hot topic for a while and then things will settle down.'

'How? When? We don't even know ourselves how things are going to settle down. Your world, Emerson, is so drastically different from my own.'

She tried not to be hurt by his words. There was no way she could forget that she'd professed her love for him while he had merely admitted that she meant a great deal to him. It wasn't the same and it wasn't equal to her feelings for him. She slowly exhaled and forced herself to remain calm. Time. He simply needed time.

'I know and I understand it may take a little while for you to get used to it, but it won't last for ever. Tomorrow some other person far more "famous" than me will do something newsworthy and we'll be forgotten.'

'Really?'

She tossed the paper aside and put her hands on either side of his face. 'Trust me, Dart.'

'You I trust. Everyone else in the world—forget about it.'

'And that's what we'll do. We'll forget about them tonight and enjoy ourselves.' She kissed him. 'Everything will turn out fine.' Even as she said the words out loud, Emmy fervently hoped she was right, that the lifestyle she'd been born into wouldn't scare off the man of her dreams.

As they drove through the streets of Sydney, Emmy promising to take him to some of her favourite spots, Dart was determined to let go of everything and just enjoy being with her. He'd known all along that she was a woman who was on the press top-ten lists, a person of interest, and as he was with her, *he* was becoming a person the press was interested in. It made him highly uncomfortable. Even sitting in the back of this amazing car made him feel out of his depth, out of his comfort zone.

Dart put both his arms around her, drawing her closer, inhaling her scent and forcing himself to remain calm. It was different and it was Emerson's world, not his. He had known things would be different when they returned to Australia, just hadn't expected things to be *this* different. He had no idea what the night was going to contain but the fact that he could hold Emmy close went a long way to helping him deal with the prying eyes they would no doubt encounter.

When they reached their destination, it was to find they were at Manly, near where the ferry docked. They left the limousine and quickly ran to board the Manly ferry, which would take them into the city, going between the Sydney Harbour Bridge and Opera House, docking at Circular Quay. Being night-time, everything was lit up, glowing brightly, and Dart did appreciate its beauty. It was nothing, however, in comparison to the way Emmy's face lit up with delight at being able to show him around.

They stood at the rail, looking out across the water, Emmy pointing out interesting landmarks and recounting memories while Dart looked at her. 'Isn't it lovely?' she asked, turning to face him.

'Absolutely.'

Emmy blushed shyly. 'Dart, you're not even looking at the sights.'

'Yes, I am.' He leaned forward. 'I'm looking at the most important sight to me.' He brushed his lips against hers, unable to get enough of this incredible woman. After the ferry docked, they took a taxi to Darling Harbour, content just to be with each other. Dart was just starting to feel a little more relaxed when a flash went off behind them. He turned and looked over his shoulder and, sure enough, there was a photographer.

'Just ignore him,' Emmy said softly, having felt Dart's arm tighten around her shoulders. On the short monorail trip to Darling Harbour they received quite a few interested glances and Dart was sure he heard one woman whisper, 'Isn't that Emerson Jofille? The socialite?'

He clenched his jaw and tucked his emotions deep down inside. As they strolled around the science museum, a few people even stopped Emmy and asked to have a photograph taken with her. Dart politely refused to join in.

'Things will settle down,' Emmy said again as they entered a small, quiet Italian restaurant. The owner greeted her with such friendliness that Dart gathered the impression she ate here quite often.

When she introduced him, the owner clasped his hands warmly.

'Dr Freeman, we are honoured to have you and dear Emmy as our guests tonight. Come. I have a quiet table where you will not be bothered.' As they were led to a candlelit table near the rear of the restaurant, Dart couldn't help but notice there were quite a few other well-known people eating there—politicians and stars of the stage and screen.

'See? We're not the most important people in the world,' Emmy pointed out once they were left alone, sipping glasses of excellent wine. She took his hand in hers. 'Just the most important to each other.'

Dart slowly found himself relaxing and even when other patrons came over to greet Emmy quite warmly, he wasn't annoyed. After enjoying a fantastic meal, being invited back to the kitchen to personally thank the chefs—something he'd never done in his life—Dart started to think that perhaps he and Emmy could make a go of a relationship after all.

They sneaked out through the rear kitchen door into a back alley filled with bins and scraps. *'Voilà!'* Emmy waved her hand with a flourish as she stepped over cabbage leaves on the ground. 'I give you the *real* lifestyles of the rich and famous.'

'It most certainly is different,' Dart agreed, slipping his arm around her shoulders and drawing her close to him. As they headed out of the alley, back to the main streets, Emmy once more pointing things out, Dart started to become aware that they were being followed. When he glanced over his shoulder, he saw that there were at least four men, all with cameras around their necks, dogging their steps.

'Em,' he said, interrupting what she was saying. 'We have company.'

Emmy sighed. 'It's not usually this difficult for me to enjoy a night out.' She spoke quietly. 'I'm sorry, Dart. Best we deal with them and give them what they want.' She slowed her steps.

'What do they want?'

'Pictures? Interviews? The juicy details on who you are and what you do.'

'*I'm* not the person of interest here. You are.' The tightness was back in his body, the annoyance returning to his tone. Emmy knew she couldn't expect miracles in one night and where she thought he'd been nice and relaxed in the restaurant, perhaps coming to see that this was indeed her life, she wondered whether it hadn't been the calm before the storm.

When she turned to face the paparazzi, Dart dropped his arm from her shoulders, shoving his hands into the pockets of his jeans. Emmy felt instantly sad and bereft at the way he was withdrawing from her, not only in a physical sense but also on an emotional level.

'Hi.' She pasted on a smile for the cameras, stepping slightly in front of Dart in order to shield him from the flashes that were now going off, left, right and centre. 'How are you all tonight?' she asked in that polite tone Dart had heard her use on several occasions.

As he watched her talk to the photo-journalists, listening to the way she evasively answered their questions, laughing with them and giving them what they wanted without really revealing a thing, Dart felt completely out of his depth.

This was Emerson's world. Emerson-Rose Jofille, socialite, television presenter and daughter to business mogul Sebastian Jofille. She wasn't his Emmy. Here, in her beloved Sydney, she couldn't be the woman she'd revealed to him in Tarparnii. With him by her side she'd be in the papers more than ever and while he felt so uncomfortable now as the flashes continued to go off, the journalists more than a little curious about him and how he fitted into Emmy's life, the earlier sense he'd had that they might be able to work out a future started to disappear.

This was Emerson's world. Not his.

As her driver Tom pulled the car up at the rear of his hotel, Dart turned to look at Emmy.

'Sorry to cut the night short,' he said. They were sitting side by side in the rear of the limo. Dart wanted space to figure things out and wrap his head around the events of this crazy evening. 'I know there were more things you wanted to show me.'

'It's fine.' She wished he'd draw her close; she wished she wasn't able to read the 'stay back' sign above his head so clearly.

'You're lying,' he said easily and without malice. 'I can tell because you're wearing your polite smile, but thank you anyway.'

'I guess tonight didn't go exactly as I'd planned. I'm sorry, Dart. I didn't realise we'd get that much interest.' How many times did she need to apologise for being who she was? It wasn't as though she'd *planned* to have the paparazzi follow them around.

'Perhaps you always have that many photographers trailing after you and you're simply used to it. You handle them very well.'

She shrugged, not wanting his praise but wanting his arms about her, his mouth on hers, so she could lose herself in the sensations they created. She also wanted his reassurance that he would stick around, that he'd wait out the inquisitive storm of the general public and choose to be with her. 'I've been raised to handle them well.' Her tone was again polite.

He nodded. 'OK.' Neither of them moved. Neither of them spoke. The space around them filled with an uncomfortable silence.

'Dart?'

'I'd better go.'

They spoke in unison and before Dart put his hand on the doorhandle, he leaned over and pressed a kiss to her lips. 'Thanks for an…interesting night.'

'Dart?' Emmy couldn't help herself and reached out to grab his arm. 'Will I see you tomorrow?' She hated the way he was making her feel, hated it that she wasn't in control of her emotions.

'I'll be at PMA again for most of the day—paperwork.'

'After that? We'll do something quiet. Together. The two of us.'

'Hmm.' He sounded as though he didn't believe her. 'Bye.' He kissed her again and this time climbed from the limo and shut the door.

Emmy sat there for a moment, biting her lip, her mind working quickly. She loved Dart and she was almost sure he loved her back but was too apprehensive to admit it. She needed to find a way to prove to him that she was serious about being with him, serious about finding a way they could be together where they could both be themselves with no paparazzi, no passers-by asking for photographs and no journalists bugging them for interviews.

After a moment she picked up her mobile phone and pressed a speed-dial number. As she waited for the person to pick up the phone, she slid the partition down between herself and her driver.

'The Blue Room wine bar, please, Tom,' she instructed. 'Ah, Felix,' she said as her call was answered. 'Can we meet?'

* * *

Dart headed to his room, startled when the hotel manager, Mr Pfeiffer, appeared at his side again.

'You're back earlier than expected, Dr Freeman,' the man said. 'I've taken the liberty of moving you to one of our more elite rooms. This way, if you please, sir.'

Dart stopped dead in his tracks. 'You did what?'

The hotel manager faltered. 'We've upgraded your room, sir. I've had the concierge move your belongings. Don't worry, nothing was damaged. I supervised the entire event.'

Dart clenched his teeth and closed his eyes, unable to believe what was happening. He opened his eyes, about to demand they put everything back into the room he'd booked when a photographer came along the hotel corridor and snapped his picture. 'Lead the way,' he said, his priority now to lock himself away from all prying eyes.

The instant his hotel room door closed behind him, Dart leaned against it, flicking the plastic key-card onto the desk. There were fresh flowers in vases on every table, the room almost smelt like a florist's. There was champagne chilling and a box of chocolates with little complimentary cards attached. No doubt the hotel manager had expected him to return with Emerson in tow.

Dart pushed this crazy night to the back of his mind and headed to the bed, kicking off his shoes. He slumped down and flicked on the television, willing to watch anything so long as it took his mind off his immediate dilemma.

The one thing he'd realised tonight, even after seeing Emmy in her world, and realising that he didn't belong there, was that he was definitely in love with her—the way she made him feel during their conversations, the way she touched his hand, the way she snuggled into him, the way she filled the void in his life. What he felt for her was stronger than anything he'd felt before, even for Marta, and that surprised him.

He loved Emerson-Rose and that only gave him bigger problems to deal with.

When he woke, to a knock at the door, it was to find the television still on and him still dressed in his clothes from last night.

The knock at the door came again, this time accompanied by the call of 'Room Service'.

Dart flicked off the television and headed to the door. 'I didn't order any—' he started to say as he opened the door, but in came a waiter, wheeling a small table with silver food covers. Dart stopped talking, waiting for the waiter to do his job of setting things up, a curious glint in the young man's eyes as he personally handed Dart a morning tabloid paper.

'Have a good breakfast, Dr Freeman,' the waiter said before disappearing.

Dart threw the paper down on the bed, barely glancing at it, but a second later he did a double-take, eyes widening as the photograph on the front page caught his attention. The phone on the desk started to ring but he ignored it.

The words 'Emmy's Love Triangle' were blazoned across the front of the paper. Below were two pictures. One was of Emmy and himself as they'd exited the Italian restaurant and the other was of Emmy sitting at a flashy Sydney bar, drink in her hand, smiling engagingly at another man.

CHAPTER THIRTEEN

EMERSON thanked the woman at the airport check-in desk before hitching her bag more firmly onto her shoulder. She was clutching her boarding pass. She walked to the boarding gate and sat down in a chair, not seeing anyone around her, not caring. Two full days had passed since she'd dropped Dart off at his hotel and she hadn't heard one word from him.

When she'd contacted the hotel the following morning after their date, she'd been informed by the manager himself that Dr Freeman had checked out. Emerson had been shocked and without asking anything else had disconnected the call. Where was he? Why hadn't he said anything to her? She didn't know if Dart had a cellphone or not. She didn't know where he lived in Brisbane or how to contact him other than through PMA. They'd been so wrapped up in each other they hadn't even exchanged basic information.

So she'd called PMA, only to be told that Dr

Freeman had cancelled his appointments for the next few days and had headed back to Brisbane. Even though Emerson had received clearance from PMA to work in Tarparnii and even though she was a well-known celebrity, PMA weren't legally able to pass on Dart's contact information. They could, however, pass on a message for him to call her.

After she'd put down the phone, completely perplexed, confused and very hurt about Dart's sudden departure from Sydney, she'd picked up the morning tabloid and had nearly hyperventilated from the shock at what was splattered across the front page.

'"Emmy's love triangle"?' She didn't even bother to scan the article, the pictures told her enough. Dart had probably taken one look at that and all but sprinted to the airport. Not only was he on the front page of the paper, the picture of her with Felix looked as though she'd gone from one man to the next.

Emmy had called PMA, had been assured that a message had been sent through to Dr Freeman. She'd received no call in return. She'd called three teaching hospitals in the Brisbane area and had finally found the one where Dart was a consultant.

Thinking she'd hit the jackpot, she'd been told that Dr Freeman was unable to take her calls and that a message would be passed to him.

That was two whole days ago and now Emmy had had enough of him not returning her calls and was taking matters into her own hands. She was going to Brisbane, to sit stubbornly in the hospital until Dart agreed to talk to her.

'Miss Jofille?'

Emmy looked up at the flight attendant, bringing her thoughts back to the present. 'Yes?'

'Are you all right?' The woman held out a tissue to Emmy and it was only then that she realised she had tears rolling down her cheeks.

'Uh…' Emmy accepted the tissue and dabbed at her eyes. 'Thank you. Sorry. Just thinking.'

'They don't seem to have been happy thoughts.' The woman's tone was sympathetic and Emmy knew she didn't have to say anything. Her life, or her life according to the media, had been a hot topic for the gossips for the past few days.'Here,' the woman said. 'Come with me.' She led Emmy to a small room with a little kitchenette. 'You can sit in here and wait, if you like. I'll come and get you once the plane is ready for boarding.'

'You're very kind. Thank you.'

'My pleasure. Help yourself to tea and coffee.' The woman smiled before closing the door and leaving Emmy alone.

Emmy sat down, feeling drained, desolated and depressed. How could Dart have left just like that? Why hadn't he given her the opportunity to at least explain the picture in the paper? Why hadn't he trusted her? Why hadn't he told her that he loved her?

A fresh bout of tears started to prick behind her eyes and she quickly sniffed them away. She'd cried enough during the past few days but had found that if she kept busy, she could keep the tears at bay. Standing, she headed to the sink and made herself a cup of tea. She'd just taken a sip when the door opened and she realised her plan to enjoy a relaxing drink in order to steady her nerves before she confronted Dart was lost.

'If you'd just like to wait in here,' Emmy could hear the same flight attendant saying. 'I'll go make sure you have a paparazzi-free path to the front of the airport.'

'I don't really care about that,' a deep male voice said. Emmy looked at the doorway, her hands starting to tremble, her breath catching in her throat, her heart trembling with a mixture of fear and excitement as she recognised that gorgeous, wonderful, sexy voice. She quickly set the cup on the sink so she didn't scald herself and turned to face Dart.

'I need to get—' Dart stopped speaking as he came further into the room and saw her standing there. 'Emmy! What are you doing here?'

'Me? What are *you* doing here?' she countered, her anger and annoyance, due to his departure, coming to the fore.

'I've come back to see you.' He frowned. 'How did you know I'd be here? I didn't tell anyone I was leaving.'

'Seems to be a habit of yours.'

'You're angry.' Dart slowly lowered his carry-on luggage to the floor and took a step closer, not even realising the flight attendant had left the room, quietly closing the door behind her. All he was conscious of was the way Emmy looked. So good. So incredible. So...*his* Emmy.

'You're darned right I'm angry. How could you just disappear like that? How could you put me through the pain of not knowing where you were?' Tears started to well rapidly in her eyes and she dabbed at them with the tissue, angry at herself for not being cool, calm and collected. 'I called the hotel only to be told that you'd checked out. PMA wouldn't pass along your details and I had no way of contacting you and…' She stopped, hiccupping over her words as she tried desperately to control the tears. She failed. Covering her face with her hands, the floodgates opened.

'Em. Oh, my Emmy.' Dart gathered her into his arms, ignoring the way she half-heartedly tried to push him away. 'You're mad at me. I get it and I'm sorry I haven't been able to return any of your phone calls.'

'Oh, so you got them,' she retorted, her words slightly muffled against his chest. She sniffed and tried to push him away but Dart refused to let her go.

'I did, but I also left word with your TV network to let them know I was called back to Brisbane. I asked them to pass the information on to you because I didn't have your cellphone number or even have a clue where you lived, apart from the fact that you have a great view of Sydney Harbour.'

'You told me you were leaving?'

'I left you a message, yes.'

'Why did you leave?' She'd at least managed to stop crying now and breathed him in, unable to believe just how much she'd missed him during the past few long and lonely days.

'I was called back to Brisbane to consult on an urgent case. The patient, a young girl of six, presented with a tropical disease that is quite common in certain parts of Tarparnii. I had it years ago so I was the perfect person to care for her. I only came out of isolation earlier this morning. The girl's fever finally broke and now she's on the mend but it's been touch and go for the past forty-eight hours.' Emmy was staring at him as though he'd hung the moon, her eyes shining brightly although slightly red from where she'd been crying.

'You left because of a medical case?'

'Yes. Why else would I leave?'

'Well…because of the photograph in the paper the other morning.' She felt his arms tighten imperceptibly about her.

'The one about Emmy's love triangle?'

'Yes.'

'You thought I was mad and that I left because you were photographed looking longingly into another man's eyes, probably a few hours after you'd dropped me at my hotel?'

'Yes.'

'Would you mind telling me who he is?'

'My accountant.'

'And you usually do business in a flashy club?' Dart tried to keep his questions fair but even he heard the slight accusatory note in his tone.

'He's part-owner in the wine bar and I wanted to see him straight away. Felix is my accountant, Dart. Has been for years. Nothing more.' Her words were urgent.

Dart absorbed this, needing more than anything to believe her. Her hands were resting on his chest, her face tipped up to look at him, and as he looked down, he knew she spoke the truth. 'Your business was that urgent that you needed to see him at the club? It couldn't wait until morning?'

'No. It couldn't, and if you must know, I was organising a present for you.' Emmy eased out of his arms, confused and annoyed and generally exhausted.

'A present?' He relaxed his hold and let her go. 'You don't need to get me a present, Emerson. I don't care about your money. I don't want any of it.'

'It's not that sort of present, Dart. Give me a little more credit for knowing the man I'm in love with.'

His breath caught at her words. 'You still love me?'

'Of course I do, you dolt. I've told you a thousand times before, the love I have for you is going to last for ever. There is only one man for me—you.' She jabbed a finger in his direction. 'I'm not so frivolous that I fall in and out of love that easily, Dartagnan Free—'

In a split second Dart had stepped close to her again and hauled her into his arms, effectively silencing her rant by pressing his mouth to hers. She tasted so good, so right, so perfect. As his mouth moved hungrily over hers, as he unleashed the pain and impatience and frustration he'd been living with for the past few days, wondering whether there was any truth to the newspaper headline, Dart was overcome by pure possessiveness.

'You taste so sweet, so good, so lovely, my Emmy,' he breathed as he pressed hot kisses to her mouth, her nose, her forehead and her eyes, before returning to plunder her mouth once more. His heart was full to bursting with the love he'd kept locked away for so long but now he could share it, he could show her, he could become whole again.

'You're my saving grace, Emmy. I never thought I could ever love again, that I would ever be able to open my heart, to let someone into my life, to trust them so completely, but I did—I have.' Dart eased back, her hands loosening at his neck to slide down his chest, her fingers splayed as though she simply couldn't get enough of him either.

'I love you, Emmy. So very much.'

Emmy couldn't help but giggle. 'It's about time you said those three little words.'

'You've been very patient.'

'I knew it couldn't be easy for you. The past can be a tricky thing to let go of, to take that chance and move forward into the future.'

'I couldn't have moved forward without you. There will always be a place for Marta in my heart but you, my elegant Emerson-Rose, are my world.'

'I am?'

'Yes. If you want me to move to Sydney, I will.'

'Really?' Emmy eased back a little to look at him more carefully to ensure he really did mean what he said.

'You don't seem to understand, Em. The past

few days, being back in Australia, being without you…' He shook his head. 'Being stuck in isolation at the hospital with no means of contacting you almost killed me. Where I thought I'd been lonely before, I was almost panicking at the thought that I'd lost you. I was determined to come here, to tell you my true feelings, to let you know I was willing to put up with the paparazzi, to make sacrifices, so long as I could be with you for the rest of my life.'

Emmy was stunned by the power of his words. 'For the rest of your life?' she whispered.

'Yes.'

'But that means…'

'Yes.' Without letting her go, needing to keep her close, Dart slipped his hand into the pocket of his trousers and pulled out a small, old-fashioned ring box.

'Oh,' Emmy gasped, and covered her mouth with one hand.

'Open it,' he instructed softly, and bent to place a quick kiss on her lips. She tried to take it but her hands were shaking so much that Dart had to reluctantly release her in order to help her. 'It was my grandmother's. She and my grandfather were married for sixty-three years.'

'Wow.' Emmy's vision was blurred with tears of happiness.

'I think that's a good start for us.' He carefully removed the old-fashioned ring with a white-gold band, filigree work on the sides and one solitaire diamond in the centre of a white-gold rose. 'I hope you like it. I can get you something different if you—'

'Don't you dare,' she said quickly. 'It's perfect. It's family history. It's personal.'

'It is.' Dart slid the ring onto her finger and looked lovingly into her eyes. 'I love you, Em. Please marry me? Be with me for ever because without you, the void in my life is impossible to fill. I need you.'

'Dart. Oh, my glorious man.' She pressed her mouth to his. 'Yes,' she murmured against his lips. 'I'll marry you. I love you so completely. No one else makes me feel the way you do. *No one.*'

Dart couldn't believe how incredibly happy he felt. An enormous weight had been lifted off his shoulders and his heart felt light after being closed for so long. And it was all thanks to his gorgeous Emmy, his gorgeous Emmy with the most delectable mouth...

'There are still a few things we need to discuss,' he said a while later as he continued to hold her close against him. 'I'm happy to move to Sydney.'

'It's a nice place to live,' she agreed. 'But I have no qualms about moving either.'

'You're very good at what you do,' Dart said. 'What about your job with the studio?'

'It's just a job, Dart. Sure, showing the public Tarparnii, as well as the needs of other developing countries, is important but I'm not the only person who can do the job.' She looked up at him. 'Home is where the heart is…and you have my heart.'

Dart looked down at the woman he loved. 'Are you saying you'll quit your job and move to Brisbane?'

'I'll change jobs and move anywhere you are. Brisbane, the country, the outback, Tarparnii. I know how to adapt, Dart. Years of training with my mother has at least taught me that much.'

He nodded. 'You most certainly do know how to adapt. You're truly gifted in that area while I…' He exhaled harshly. 'I don't have a clue where I fit. I feel disjointed wherever I am, except when I'm standing still with you in my arms.'

He smiled at her and pressed a kiss to her lips. 'I work for six months at a hospital in Brisbane, all the while counting the days until I can return to Tarparnii.'

'Then why don't we go to Tarparnii?'

'But PMA has rules.'

'Let's see if we can't…alter them a little.' She nodded encouragingly. Dart looked at the woman before him, seeing that she was deadly serious.

'You're serious?' He laughed. 'You are.'

Emmy's blue gaze was intent. 'Why can't we change things? What if we go to Tarparnii contracted not only to run but also to build a surgery and set it up. I'm talking about a real dedicated building with running water, not a bamboo hut. Think of how it will help Meeree and Jalak in their village. And in J'tagnan's village, we could build another one.' Emmy was becoming excited about the possibilities.

'All of that takes money, investment backers.'

She spread her arms wide and angled her head to the side. 'Why do you think I was meeting Felix?'

'That's why you were meeting him?'

'I could see the other night that you weren't comfortable with the paparazzi and even though you're willing to put up with them, that's no sort of lifestyle for our new life together. I met Felix to get him to crunch some numbers, to see if it's doable.'

'Obviously it is.'

'It is.' She laughed and he knew he'd never get tired of hearing that sound. 'This is going to work.'

'Just like that?'

'Why not?'

Dart was astounded. 'You'd finance it?'

'Most of it. I have trust funds from my parents and both sets of grandparents. I don't need them, Dart. Money has brought me nothing but misery for most of my life so, yes, I think these projects will definitely work. My brother's already on board and two of his colleagues are showing interest.'

'You've been busy these past few days.'

'I wanted to have your present ready to give you when I came to Brisbane to see you.'

'You were really going to come?'

'I was going to wait in a hospital waiting room, drinking vending-machine coffee, until you agreed to talk to me. Instead, you've come to find me.'

'My heart belongs with yours, Em. Always will.' Dart's mouth settled over hers and Emmy had never felt better in her life.

She was finally home, in the place where she'd always belonged, in Dart's arms, for evermore.

EPILOGUE

Two years later, Emmy sat looking out of the plane window at Sydney Harbour below. They were coming home to Australia and she was surprised not to get that same excited feeling she'd had on previous occasions whenever she'd been away from her country.

She looked across at her husband, who was pretending to snooze, his head back, his eyes closed. That's when the excited feelings started tingling within her. Her husband, being with him, staying together, that was where her happiness came from now and it was just the way she wanted it.

They were returning to Sydney for her brother's wedding after spending the past eighteen months working in Tarparnii, erecting clinic buildings, complete with running water and proper examination beds rather than stretchers, in several villages. There was still a lot of work to do but she and Dart had trained other PMA personnel and soon, after the wedding, they were looking forward to relocating themselves to Cairns, in far north Queensland.

'It's close to Tarparnii, the climate is similar and I've never lived there before so we can make fresh memories. Our memories,' Dart had said, and kissed her.

Now Emmy couldn't wait for the wedding to be over. Tristan had gone the road of the big society wedding, which was just fine for him. Emmy and Dart had been married on a golden-sand beach at sunrise, no press, no fanfare, just the two of them with a few of their close friends, Emmy's camera crew taping the ceremony for posterity. Their *real* wedding had taken place in Tarparnii, with their PMA friends around them for the *par'Mach* festival, which was where the Tarparniian women chose their life partners. There, she and Dart had been bound together for all eternity.

A smile touched her lips as she twirled the plain gold wedding band she'd worn for almost two years before she entwined her hand with Dart's strong, lean fingers…fingers that knew every part of her body, knowing just where to touch, to excite, to love.

He opened his eyes. 'Are we almost there?'

'We are. Four days of press, of interviews, of

smiling until your cheek muscles hurt. The paparazzi are going to be all over this wedding.'

Dart shrugged. 'Good for the paparazzi. I'm more concerned about you.' He reached over and touched her stomach with his free hand, caressing her belly and knowing her pregnancy would soon start to show. For now, though, he loved it that it was just their secret.

She relaxed at his words, glad he'd now accepted that from time to time the press would invade their privacy. It didn't last for ever, though. 'I'll be fine.'

'I'll make sure you are.'

She leaned up and kissed him. '*My* protector.'

'For ever, *my* Emerson-Rose.'

MEDICAL™

Large Print

Titles for the next six months…

July

SHEIKH, CHILDREN'S DOCTOR…HUSBAND	Meredith Webber
SIX-WEEK MARRIAGE MIRACLE	Jessica Matthews
RESCUED BY THE DREAMY DOC	Amy Andrews
NAVY OFFICER TO FAMILY MAN	Emily Forbes
ST PIRAN'S: ITALIAN SURGEON, FORBIDDEN BRIDE	Margaret McDonagh
THE BABY WHO STOLE THE DOCTOR'S HEART	Dianne Drake

August

CEDAR BLUFF'S MOST ELIGIBLE BACHELOR	Laura Iding
DOCTOR: DIAMOND IN THE ROUGH	Lucy Clark
BECOMING DR BELLINI'S BRIDE	Joanna Neil
MIDWIFE, MOTHER…ITALIAN'S WIFE	Fiona McArthur
ST PIRAN'S: DAREDEVIL, DOCTOR…DAD!	Anne Fraser
SINGLE DAD'S TRIPLE TROUBLE	Fiona Lowe

September

SUMMER SEASIDE WEDDING	Abigail Gordon
REUNITED: A MIRACLE MARRIAGE	Judy Campbell
THE MAN WITH THE LOCKED AWAY HEART	Melanie Milburne
SOCIALITE…OR NURSE IN A MILLION?	Molly Evans
ST PIRAN'S: THE BROODING HEART SURGEON	Alison Roberts
PLAYBOY DOCTOR TO DOTING DAD	Sue MacKay

MILLS & BOON

MEDICAL™

Large Print

October

TAMING DR TEMPEST	Meredith Webber
THE DOCTOR AND THE DEBUTANTE	Anne Fraser
THE HONOURABLE MAVERICK	Alison Roberts
THE UNSUNG HERO	Alison Roberts
ST PIRAN'S: THE FIREMAN AND NURSE LOVEDAY	Kate Hardy
FROM BROODING BOSS TO ADORING DAD	Dianne Drake

November

HER LITTLE SECRET	Carol Marinelli
THE DOCTOR'S DAMSEL IN DISTRESS	Janice Lynn
THE TAMING OF DR ALEX DRAYCOTT	Joanna Neil
THE MAN BEHIND THE BADGE	Sharon Archer
ST PIRAN'S: TINY MIRACLE TWINS	Maggie Kingsley
MAVERICK IN THE ER	Jessica Matthews

December

FLIRTING WITH THE SOCIETY DOCTOR	Janice Lynn
WHEN ONE NIGHT ISN'T ENOUGH	Wendy S. Marcus
MELTING THE ARGENTINE DOCTOR'S HEART	Meredith Webber
SMALL TOWN MARRIAGE MIRACLE	Jennifer Taylor
ST PIRAN'S: PRINCE ON THE CHILDREN'S WARD	Sarah Morgan
HARRY ST CLAIR: ROGUE OR DOCTOR?	Fiona McArthur